THE
ALCHEMIST

Also by Paulo Coelho

The Pilgrimage

The Valkyries

By the River Piedra I Sat Down and Wept

The Fifth Mountain

Veronika Decides to Die

The Devil and Miss Prym

Manual of the Warrior of Light

Eleven Minutes

The Zahir

Like the Flowing River

The Witch of Portobello

Brida

The Winner Stands Alone

Aleph

Manuscript Found in Accra

THE
ALCHEMIST

**A FABLE ABOUT FOLLOWING
YOUR DREAM**

Paulo Coelho

HARPER

HARPER

An imprint of HarperCollins*Publishers*
77–85 Fulham Palace Road
Hammersmith, London W6 8JB

www.harpercollins.co.uk
www.paulocoelho.com

First published by Editora Rocco Ltd 1988
English edition 1993
This HarperCollins edition published 2012

27

A catalogue record for this book
is available from the British Library

ISBN 978-0-0071-5566-8

Printed and bound in Great Britain by
Clays Ltd, St Ives plc

MIX
Paper from
responsible sources
FSC **FSC™ C007454**

Author's Note

I remember receiving a letter from the American publisher, HarperCollins, which said that "reading *The Alchemist* was like getting up at dawn and seeing the sun rise while the rest of the world still slept." I went outside, looked up at the sky and thought to myself, "So, the book is going to be translated!" At the time, I was struggling to establish myself as a writer and to follow my path, despite all the voices telling me it was impossible.

And little by little, my dream was becoming reality. Ten, a hundred, a thousand, a million copies were sold in America. One day, a Brazilian journalist phoned to say that President Clinton had been photographed reading the book. Some time later, when I was in Turkey, I opened the magazine *Vanity Fair* and there was Julia Roberts, declaring that she adored the book. Walking alone down a street in Miami, I heard a girl telling her mother, "You must read *The Alchemist*!"

The book has been translated into 74 languages, has sold more than 65 million copies worldwide, and people are beginning to ask: "What's the secret behind such a huge success?" The only honest response is that I don't know. All I know is that, like Santiago the shepherd boy, we all need to be aware of our personal calling.

Paulo Coelho

What is a personal calling? It is God's blessing, it is the path that God chose for you here on Earth. Whenever we do something that fills us with enthusiasm, we are following our legend. However, we don't all have the courage to confront our own dream. Why?

There are four obstacles. First, we are told from childhood onwards that everything we want to do is impossible. We grow up with this idea, and as the years accumulate, so too do the layers of prejudice, fear and guilt. There comes a time when our personal calling is so deeply buried in our soul as to be invisible. But it's still there.

If we have the courage to disinter our dream, we are then faced by the second obstacle: love. We know what we want to do, but are afraid of hurting those around us by abandoning everything in order to pursue our dream. We do not realize that love is just a further impetus, not something that will prevent us going forward, and that those who genuinely wish us well want us to be happy and are prepared to accompany us on that journey.

Once we have accepted that love is a stimulus, we come up against the third obstacle: fear of the defeats we will meet on the path. We who fight for our dream suffer far more when it doesn't work out, because we cannot fall back on the old excuse, "Oh, well, I didn't really want it anyway." We do want it and know that we have staked everything on it and that the path of the personal calling is no easier than any other path, except that our whole heart is in this journey. Then we warriors of light must be prepared to have patience in difficult times and to know that the Universe is conspiring in our favor, even though we may not understand how.

I ask myself: are defeats necessary? Well, necessary or not, they happen. When we first begin fighting for our dream, we have no experience and make many mistakes. The secret of life, though, is to fall seven times and to get up eight times.

So, why is it so important to live our personal calling if we are only going to suffer more than other people? Because once we have overcome the defeats — and we always do — we are filled with a greater sense of euphoria and confidence. In the silence of our hearts, we know that we are proving ourselves worthy of the miracle of life. Each day, each hour, is part of the good fight. We start to live with enthusiasm and pleasure. Intense, unexpected suffering passes more quickly than suffering that is apparently bearable; the latter goes on for years and, without our noticing, eats away at our soul, until, one day, we are no longer able to free ourselves from the bitterness and it stays with us for the rest of our lives.

Having disinterred our dream, having used the power of love to nurture it and spent many years living with the scars, we suddenly notice that what we always wanted is there, waiting for us, perhaps the very next day. Then comes the fourth obstacle: the fear of realizing the dream for which we have been fighting all our lives.

Oscar Wilde said, "Each man kills the thing he loves." And it's true. The mere possibility of getting what we want fills the soul of the ordinary person with guilt. We look around at all those who have failed to get what they want and feel that we do not deserve to get what we want either. We forget about all the obstacles we overcame, all the suffering we endured, all the things we had to give up in order to get this far. I have known a lot of people who, when their personal calling was within their grasp, went on to commit a series of stupid mistakes and never reached their goal when it was only a step away.

This is the most dangerous of the obstacles because it has a kind of saintly aura about it: renouncing joy and conquest. But if you believe yourself worthy of the thing you fought so hard to get, then you become an instrument of God, you help the Soul of the World, and you understand why you are here.

Translated by Margaret Jull Costa

Prologue

The alchemist picked up a book that someone in the caravan had bought. Leafing through the pages, he found a story about Narcissus.

The alchemist knew the legend of Narcissus, a youth who knelt daily beside a lake to contemplate his own beauty. He was so fascinated by himself that, one morning, he fell into the lake and drowned. At the spot where he fell, a flower was born, which was called the narcissus.

But this was not how the author of the book ended the story.

He said that when Narcissus died, the goddesses of the forest appeared and found the lake, which had been fresh water, transformed into a lake of salty tears.

"Why do you weep?" the goddesses asked.

"I weep for Narcissus," the lake replied.

"Ah, it is no surprise that you weep for Narcissus," they said, "for though we always pursued him in the forest, you alone could contemplate his beauty close at hand."

"But … was Narcissus beautiful?" the lake asked.

"Who better than you to know that?" the goddesses said in wonder. "After all, it was by your banks that he knelt each day to contemplate himself!"

The lake was silent for some time. Finally, it said:

"I weep for Narcissus, but I never noticed that Narcissus was beautiful. I weep because, each time he knelt beside my banks, I could see, in the depths of his eyes, my own beauty reflected."

"What a lovely story," the alchemist thought.

Translated by Clifford E. Landers

Part One

The boy's name was Santiago. Dusk was falling as the boy arrived with his herd at an abandoned church. The roof had fallen in long ago, and an enormous sycamore had grown on the spot where the sacristy had once stood.

He decided to spend the night there. He saw to it that all the sheep entered through the ruined gate, and then laid some planks across it to prevent the flock from wandering away during the night. There were no wolves in the region, but once an animal had strayed during the night, and the boy had had to spend the entire next day searching for it.

He swept the floor with his jacket and lay down, using the book he had just finished reading as a pillow. He told himself that he would have to start reading thicker books: they lasted longer, and made more comfortable pillows.

It was still dark when he awoke, and, looking up, he could see the stars through the half-destroyed roof.

I wanted to sleep a little longer, he thought. He had had the same dream that night as a week ago, and once again he had awakened before it ended.

He arose and, taking up his crook, began to awaken the sheep that still slept. He had noticed that, as soon as he awoke, most of his animals also began to stir. It was as if some mysterious energy bound his life to that of the sheep, with whom he had spent the past two years, leading them through the countryside in search of food and water. "They are so used to me that they know my schedule," he muttered. Thinking about that for a moment, he realized that it could be the other way around: that it was he who had become accustomed to *their* schedule.

But there were certain of them who took a bit longer to awaken. The boy prodded them, one by one, with his crook, calling each by name. He had always believed that the sheep were able to understand what he said. So there were times when he read them parts of his books that had made an impression on him, or when he would tell them of the loneliness or the happiness of a shepherd in the fields. Sometimes he would comment to them on the things he had seen in the villages they passed.

But for the past few days he had spoken to them about only one thing: the girl, the daughter of a merchant who lived in the village they would reach in about four days. He had been to the village only once, the year before. The merchant was the proprietor of a dry goods shop, and he always demanded that the sheep be sheared in his presence, so that he would not be cheated. A friend had told the boy about the shop, and he had taken his sheep there.

* * *

"I need to sell some wool," the boy told the merchant.

The shop was busy, and the man asked the shepherd to wait until the afternoon. So the boy sat on the steps of the shop and took a book from his bag.

"I didn't know shepherds knew how to read," said a girl's voice behind him.

The girl was typical of the region of Andalusia, with flowing black hair, and eyes that vaguely recalled the Moorish conquerors.

"Well, usually I learn more from my sheep than from books," he answered. During the two hours that they talked, she told him she was the merchant's daughter, and spoke of life in the village, where each day was like all the others. The shepherd told her of the Andalusian countryside, and related the news from the other towns where he had stopped. It was a pleasant change from talking to his sheep.

"How did you learn to read?" the girl asked at one point.

"Like everybody learns," he said. "In school."

"Well, if you know how to read, why are you just a shepherd?"

The boy mumbled an answer that allowed him to avoid responding to her question. He was sure the girl would never understand. He went on telling stories about his travels, and her bright, Moorish eyes went wide with fear and surprise. As the time passed, the boy found himself wishing that the day would never end, that her father would stay busy and keep him waiting for three days. He recognized that he was feeling something he had never experienced before: the desire to live in one place forever. With the girl with the raven hair, his days would never be the same again.

But finally the merchant appeared, and asked the boy to shear four sheep. He paid for the wool and asked the shepherd to come back the following year.

*   *   *

And now it was only four days before he would be back in that same village. He was excited, and at the same time uneasy: maybe the girl had already forgotten him. Lots of shepherds passed through, selling their wool.

"It doesn't matter," he said to his sheep. "I know other girls in other places."

But in his heart he knew that it did matter. And he knew that shepherds, like seamen and like traveling salesmen, always found a town where there was someone who could make them forget the joys of carefree wandering.

The day was dawning, and the shepherd urged his sheep in the direction of the sun. They never have to make any decisions, he thought. Maybe that's why they always stay close to me.

The only things that concerned the sheep were food and water. As long as the boy knew how to find the best pastures in Andalusia, they would be his friends. Yes, their days were all the same, with the seemingly endless hours between sunrise and dusk; and they had never read a book in their young lives, and didn't understand when the boy told them about the sights of the cities. They were content with just food and water, and, in exchange, they generously gave of their wool, their company, and — once in a while — their meat.

If I became a monster today, and decided to kill them, one by one, they would become aware only after most of the flock had been slaughtered, thought the boy. They trust me, and they've forgotten how to rely on their own instincts, because I lead them to nourishment.

The boy was surprised at his thoughts. Maybe the church, with the sycamore growing from within, had been haunted. It had caused him to have the same dream for a second time, and it was causing him to feel anger toward his faithful companions. He drank a bit from the wine that remained from his dinner of the night before, and he gathered his jacket closer to his body. He knew that a few hours from now, with the sun at its zenith, the heat would be so great that he would not be able to lead his flock across the fields. It was the time of day when all of Spain slept during the summer. The heat lasted until nightfall, and all that time he had to carry his jacket. But when he thought to complain about the burden of its weight, he remembered that, because he had the jacket, he had withstood the cold of the dawn.

We have to be prepared for change, he thought, and he was grateful for the jacket's weight and warmth.

The jacket had a purpose, and so did the boy. His purpose in life was to travel, and, after two years of

walking the Andalusian terrain, he knew all the cities
of the region. He was planning, on this visit, to explain
to the girl how it was that a simple shepherd knew
how to read. That he had attended a seminary until
he was sixteen. His parents had wanted him to become
a priest, and thereby a source of pride for a simple
farm family. They worked hard just to have food and
water, like the sheep. He had studied Latin, Spanish,
and theology. But ever since he had been a child, he
had wanted to know the world, and this was much
more important to him than knowing God and learning about man's sins. One afternoon, on a visit to his
family, he had summoned up the courage to tell his
father that he didn't want to become a priest. That he
wanted to travel.

* * *

"People from all over the world have passed through
this village, son," said his father. "They come in search
of new things, but when they leave they are basically
the same people they were when they arrived. They
climb the mountain to see the castle, and they wind up
thinking that the past was better than what we have
now. They have blond hair, or dark skin, but basically
they're the same as the people who live right here."

"But I'd like to see the castles in the towns where
they live," the boy explained.

"Those people, when they see our land, say that they
would like to live here forever," his father continued.

"Well, I'd like to see their land, and see how they live," said his son.

"The people who come here have a lot of money to spend, so they can afford to travel," his father said. "Amongst us, the only ones who travel are the shepherds."

"Well, then I'll be a shepherd!"

His father said no more. The next day, he gave his son a pouch that held three ancient Spanish gold coins.

"I found these one day in the fields. I wanted them to be a part of your inheritance. But use them to buy your flock. Take to the fields, and someday you'll learn that our countryside is the best, and our women the most beautiful."

And he gave the boy his blessing. The boy could see in his father's gaze a desire to be able, himself, to travel the world—a desire that was still alive, despite his father's having had to bury it, over dozens of years, under the burden of struggling for water to drink, food to eat, and the same place to sleep every night of his life.

* * *

The horizon was tinged with red, and suddenly the sun appeared. The boy thought back to that conversation with his father, and felt happy; he had already seen many castles and met many women (but none the equal of the one who awaited him several days hence). He owned a jacket, a book that he could trade for another, and a flock of sheep. But, most important, he was able every day to live out his dream. If he were to tire of the Andalusian fields, he could sell his sheep and go to sea. By the time he had had enough of the sea, he would already have known other cities, other women, and other chances to be happy. I couldn't have found God in the seminary, he thought, as he looked at the sunrise.

Whenever he could, he sought out a new road to travel. He had never been to that ruined church before, in spite of having traveled through those parts many times. The world was huge and inexhaustible; he had only to allow his sheep to set the route for a while, and he would discover other interesting things. The problem is that they don't even realize that they're walking a new road every day. They don't see that the fields are new and the seasons change. All they think about is food and water.

Maybe we're all that way, the boy mused. Even me—I haven't thought of other women since I met the merchant's daughter. Looking at the sun, he calculated that he would reach Tarifa before midday. There, he could exchange his book for a thicker one, fill his wine bottle, shave, and have a haircut; he had to prepare himself for his meeting with the girl, and he didn't want to think about the possibility that some other shepherd, with a larger flock of sheep, had arrived there before him and asked for her hand.

It's the possibility of having a dream come true that makes life interesting, he thought, as he looked again at the position of the sun, and hurried his pace. He had suddenly remembered that, in Tarifa, there was an old woman who interpreted dreams.

* * *

The old woman led the boy to a room at the back of her house; it was separated from her living room by a curtain of colored beads. The room's furnishings consisted of a table, an image of the Sacred Heart of Jesus, and two chairs.

The woman sat down, and told him to be seated as well. Then she took both of his hands in hers, and began quietly to pray.

It sounded like a Gypsy prayer. The boy had already had experience on the road with Gypsies; they also traveled, but they had no flocks of sheep. People said that Gypsies spent their lives tricking others. It was also said that they had a pact with the devil, and that they kidnapped children and, taking them away to their mysterious camps, made them their slaves. As a child, the boy had always been frightened to death that he would be captured by Gypsies, and this childhood fear returned when the old woman took his hands in hers.

But she has the Sacred Heart of Jesus there, he thought, trying to reassure himself. He didn't want his hand to begin trembling, showing the old woman that he was fearful. He recited an Our Father silently.

"Very interesting," said the woman, never taking her eyes from the boy's hands, and then she fell silent.

The boy was becoming nervous. His hands began to tremble, and the woman sensed it. He quickly pulled his hands away.

"I didn't come here to have you read my palm," he said, already regretting having come. He thought for a moment that it would be better to pay her fee and leave without learning a thing, that he was giving too much importance to his recurrent dream.

"You came so that you could learn about your dreams," said the old woman. "And dreams are the language of God. When he speaks in our language, I can interpret what he has said. But if he speaks in the language of the soul, it is only you who can understand. But, whichever it is, I'm going to charge you for the consultation."

Another trick, the boy thought. But he decided to take a chance. A shepherd always takes his chances with wolves and with drought, and that's what makes a shepherd's life exciting.

"I have had the same dream twice," he said. "I dreamed that I was in a field with my sheep, when a child appeared and began to play with the animals. I don't like people to do that, because the sheep are afraid of strangers. But children always seem to be able to play with them without frightening them. I don't know why. I don't know how animals know the age of human beings."

"Tell me more about your dream," said the woman. "I have to get back to my cooking, and, since you don't have much money, I can't give you a lot of time."

"The child went on playing with my sheep for quite a while," continued the boy, a bit upset. "And suddenly, the child took me by both hands and transported me to the Egyptian pyramids."

He paused for a moment to see if the woman knew what the Egyptian pyramids were. But she said nothing.

"Then, at the Egyptian pyramids," — he said the last three words slowly, so that the old woman would understand — "the child said to me, 'If you come here, you will find a hidden treasure.' And, just as she was about to show me the exact location, I woke up. Both times."

The woman was silent for some time. Then she again took his hands and studied them carefully.

"I'm not going to charge you anything now," she said. "But I want one-tenth of the treasure, if you find it."

The boy laughed — out of happiness. He was going to be able to save the little money he had because of a dream about hidden treasure!

"Well, interpret the dream," he said.

"First, swear to me. Swear that you will give me one-tenth of your treasure in exchange for what I am going to tell you."

The shepherd swore that he would. The old woman asked him to swear again while looking at the image of the Sacred Heart of Jesus.

"It's a dream in the language of the world," she said. "I can interpret it, but the interpretation is very difficult. That's why I feel that I deserve a part of what you find.

"And this is my interpretation: you must go to the Pyramids in Egypt. I have never heard of them, but, if it was a child who showed them to you, they exist. There you will find a treasure that will make you a rich man."

The boy was surprised, and then irritated. He didn't need to seek out the old woman for this! But then he remembered that he wasn't going to have to pay anything.

"I didn't need to waste my time just for this," he said.

"I told you that your dream was a difficult one. It's the simple things in life that are the most extraordinary; only wise men are able to understand them. And since I am not wise, I have had to learn other arts, such as the reading of palms."

"Well, how am I going to get to Egypt?"

"I only interpret dreams. I don't know how to turn them into reality. That's why I have to live off what my daughters provide me with."

"And what if I never get to Egypt?"

"Then I don't get paid. It wouldn't be the first time."

And the woman told the boy to leave, saying she had already wasted too much time with him.

So the boy was disappointed; he decided that he would never again believe in dreams. He remembered that he had a number of things he had to take care of: he went to the market for something to eat, he traded his book for one that was thicker, and he found a bench in the plaza where he could sample the new wine he had bought. The day was hot, and the wine was refreshing. The sheep were at the gates of the city, in a stable that belonged to a friend. The boy knew a lot of people in the city. That was what made traveling appeal to him—he always made new friends, and he didn't need to spend all of his time with them. When someone sees the same people every day, as had happened with him at the seminary, they wind up becoming a part of that person's life. And then they want the person to change. If someone isn't what others want them to be, the others become angry. Everyone seems to have a clear idea of how other people should lead their lives, but none about his or her own.

He decided to wait until the sun had sunk a bit lower in the sky before following his flock back through the fields. Three days from now, he would be with the merchant's daughter.

He started to read the book he had bought. On the very first page it described a burial ceremony. And the names of the people involved were very difficult to pronounce. If he ever wrote a book, he thought, he would present one person at a time, so that the reader wouldn't have to worry about memorizing a lot of names.

When he was finally able to concentrate on what he was reading, he liked the book better; the burial was on a snowy day, and he welcomed the feeling of being cold. As he read on, an old man sat down at his side and tried to strike up a conversation.

"What are they doing?" the old man asked, pointing at the people in the plaza.

"Working," the boy answered dryly, making it look as if he wanted to concentrate on his reading.

Actually, he was thinking about shearing his sheep in front of the merchant's daughter, so that she could see that he was someone who was capable of doing difficult things. He had already imagined the scene many times; every time, the girl became fascinated when he explained that the sheep had to be sheared from back to front. He also tried to remember some good stories to relate as he sheared the sheep. Most of them he had read in books, but he would tell them as if they were from his personal experience. She would never know the difference, because she didn't know how to read.

Meanwhile, the old man persisted in his attempt to strike up a conversation. He said that he was tired and thirsty, and asked if he might have a sip of the boy's wine. The boy offered his bottle, hoping that the old man would leave him alone.

But the old man wanted to talk, and he asked the boy what book he was reading. The boy was tempted to be rude, and move to another bench, but his father had taught him to be respectful of the elderly. So he held out the book to the man — for two reasons: first, that he, himself, wasn't sure how to pronounce the title; and second, that if the old man didn't know how to read, he would probably feel ashamed and decide of his own accord to change benches.

"Hmm ..." said the old man, looking at all sides of the book, as if it were some strange object. "This is an important book, but it's really irritating."

The boy was shocked. The old man knew how to read, and had already read the book. And if the book was irritating, as the old man had said, the boy still had time to change it for another.

"It's a book that says the same thing almost all the other books in the world say," continued the old man. "It describes people's inability to choose their own destinies. And it ends up saying that everyone believes the world's greatest lie."

"What's the world's greatest lie?" the boy asked, completely surprised.

"It's this: that at a certain point in our lives, we lose control of what's happening to us, and our lives become controlled by fate. That's the world's greatest lie."

"That's never happened to me," the boy said. "They wanted me to be a priest, but I decided to become a shepherd."

"Much better," said the old man. "Because you really like to travel."

"He knew what I was thinking," the boy said to himself. The old man, meanwhile, was leafing through the book, without seeming to want to return it at all. The boy noticed that the man's clothing was strange. He looked like an Arab, which was not unusual in those parts. Africa was only a few hours from Tarifa; one had only to cross the narrow straits by boat. Arabs often appeared in the city, shopping and chanting their strange prayers several times a day.

"Where are you from?" the boy asked.

"From many places."

"No one can be from many places," the boy said. "I'm a shepherd, and I have been to many places, but I come from only one place — from a city near an ancient castle. That's where I was born."

"Well then, we could say that I was born in Salem."

The boy didn't know where Salem was, but he didn't want to ask, fearing that he would appear ignorant. He looked at the people in the plaza for a while; they were coming and going, and all of them seemed to be very busy.

"So, what is Salem like?" he asked, trying to get some sort of clue.

"It's like it always has been."

No clue yet. But he knew that Salem wasn't in Andalusia. If it were, he would already have heard of it.

"And what do you do in Salem?" he insisted.

"What do I do in Salem?" The old man laughed. "Well, I'm the king of Salem!"

People say strange things, the boy thought. Sometimes it's better to be with the sheep, who don't say anything. And better still to be alone with one's books. They tell their incredible stories at the time when you want to hear them. But when you're talking to people, they say some things that are so strange that you don't know how to continue the conversation.

"My name is Melchizedek," said the old man. "How many sheep do you have?"

"Enough," said the boy. He could see that the old man wanted to know more about his life.

"Well, then, we've got a problem. I can't help you if you feel you've got enough sheep."

The boy was getting irritated. He wasn't asking for help. It was the old man who had asked for a drink of his wine, and had started the conversation.

"Give me my book," the boy said. "I have to go and gather my sheep and get going."

"Give me one-tenth of your sheep," said the old man, "and I'll tell you how to find the hidden treasure."

The boy remembered his dream, and suddenly everything was clear to him. The old woman hadn't charged him anything, but the old man — maybe he was her husband — was going to find a way to get much more money in exchange for information about something that didn't even exist. The old man was probably a Gypsy, too.

But before the boy could say anything, the old man leaned over, picked up a stick, and began to write in the sand of the plaza. Something bright reflected from his chest with such intensity that the boy was momentarily blinded. With a movement that was too quick for someone his age, the man covered whatever it was with his cape. When his vision returned to normal, the boy was able to read what the old man had written in the sand.

There, in the sand of the plaza of that small city, the boy read the names of his father and his mother and the name of the seminary he had attended. He read the name of the merchant's daughter, which he hadn't even known, and he read things he had never told anyone.

* * *

"I'm the king of Salem," the old man had said.

"Why would a king be talking with a shepherd?" the boy asked, awed and embarrassed.

"For several reasons. But let's say that the most important is that you have succeeded in discovering your destiny."

The boy didn't know what a person's "destiny" was.

"It's what you have always wanted to accomplish. Everyone, when they are young, knows what their destiny is.

"At that point in their lives, everything is clear and everything is possible. They are not afraid to dream, and to yearn for everything they would like to see happen to them in their lives. But, as time passes, a mysterious force begins to convince them that it will be impossible for them to realize their destiny."

None of what the old man was saying made much sense to the boy. But he wanted to know what the "mysterious force" was; the merchant's daughter would be impressed when he told her about that!

"It's a force that appears to be negative, but actually shows you how to realize your destiny. It prepares your spirit and your will, because there is one great truth on this planet: whoever you are, or whatever it is that you do, when you really want something, it's because that desire originated in the soul of the universe. It's your mission on earth."

"Even when all you want to do is travel? Or marry the daughter of a textile merchant?"

"Yes, or even search for treasure. The Soul of the World is nourished by people's happiness. And also by unhappiness, envy, and jealousy. To realize one's destiny is a person's only real obligation. All things are one.

"And, when you want something, all the universe conspires in helping you to achieve it."

They were both silent for a time, observing the plaza and the townspeople. It was the old man who spoke first.

"Why do you tend a flock of sheep?"

"Because I like to travel."

The old man pointed to a baker standing in his shop window at one corner of the plaza. "When he was a child, that man wanted to travel, too. But he decided first to buy his bakery and put some money aside. When he's an old man, he's going to spend a month in Africa. He never realized that people are capable, at any time in their lives, of doing what they dream of."

"He should have decided to become a shepherd," the boy said.

"Well, he thought about that," the old man said. "But bakers are more important people than shepherds.

Bakers have homes, while shepherds sleep out in the open. Parents would rather see their children marry bakers than shepherds."

The boy felt a pang in his heart, thinking about the merchant's daughter. There was surely a baker in her town.

The old man continued, "In the long run, what people think about shepherds and bakers becomes more important for them than their own destinies."

The old man leafed through the book, and fell to reading a page he came to. The boy waited, and then interrupted the old man just as he himself had been interrupted. "Why are you telling me all this?"

"Because you are trying to realize your destiny. And you are at the point where you're about to give it all up."

"And that's when you always appear on the scene?"

"Not always in this way, but I always appear in one form or another. Sometimes I appear in the form of a solution, or a good idea. At other times, at a crucial moment, I make it easier for things to happen. There are other things I do, too, but most of the time people don't realize I've done them."

The old man related that, the week before, he had been forced to appear before a miner, and had taken the form of a stone. The miner had abandoned everything to go mining for emeralds. For five years he had been working a certain river, and had examined hundreds of thousands of stones looking for an emerald.

The miner was about to give it all up, right at the point when, if he were to examine just one more stone—just one more—he would find his emerald. Since the miner had sacrificed everything to his destiny, the old man decided to become involved. He transformed himself into a stone that rolled up to the miner's foot. The miner, with all the anger and frustration of his five fruitless years, picked up the stone and threw it aside. But he had thrown it with such force that it broke the stone it fell upon, and there, embedded in the broken stone, was the most beautiful emerald in the world.

"People learn, early in their lives, what is their reason for being," said the old man, with a certain bitterness. "Maybe that's why they give up on it so early, too. But that's the way it is."

The boy reminded the old man that he had said something about hidden treasure.

"Treasure is uncovered by the force of flowing water, and it is buried by the same currents," said the old man. "If you want to learn about your own treasure, you will have to give me one-tenth of your flock."

"What about one-tenth of my treasure?"

The old man looked disappointed. "If you start out by promising what you don't even have yet, you'll lose your desire to work toward getting it."

The boy told him that he had already promised to give one-tenth of his treasure to the Gypsy.

"Gypsies are experts at getting people to do that," sighed the old man. "In any case, it's good that you've learned that everything in life has its price. This is what the Warriors of the Light try to teach."

The old man returned the book to the boy.

"Tomorrow, at this same time, bring me a tenth of your flock. And I will tell you how to find the hidden treasure. Good afternoon."

And he vanished around the corner of the plaza.

* * *

The boy began again to read his book, but he was no longer able to concentrate. He was tense and upset, because he knew that the old man was right. He went over to the bakery and bought a loaf of bread, thinking about whether or not he should tell the baker what the old man had said about him. Sometimes it's better to leave things as they are, he thought to himself, and decided to say nothing. If he were to say anything, the baker would spend three days thinking about giving it all up, even though he had gotten used to the way things were. The boy could certainly resist causing that kind of anxiety for the baker. So he began to wander through the city, and found himself at the gates. There was a small building there, with a window at which people bought tickets to Africa. And he knew that Egypt was in Africa.

"Can I help you?" asked the man behind the window.

"Maybe tomorrow," said the boy, moving away. If he sold just one of his sheep, he'd have enough to get to the other shore of the strait. The idea frightened him.

"Another dreamer," said the ticket seller to his assistant, watching the boy walk away. "He doesn't have enough money to travel."

While standing at the ticket window, the boy had remembered his flock, and decided he should go back to being a shepherd. In two years he had learned everything about shepherding: he knew how to shear sheep, how to care for pregnant ewes, and how to protect the sheep from wolves. He knew all the fields and pastures of Andalusia. And he knew what was the fair price for every one of his animals.

He decided to return to his friend's stable by the longest route possible. As he walked past the city's castle, he interrupted his return, and climbed the stone ramp that led to the top of the wall. From there, he could see Africa in the distance. Someone had once told him that it was from there that the Moors had come, to occupy all of Spain.

He could see almost the entire city from where he sat, including the plaza where he had talked with the old man. Curse the moment I met that old man, he thought. He had come to the town only to find a woman who could interpret his dream. Neither the woman nor the old man were at all impressed by the fact that he was a shepherd. They were solitary individuals who no longer believed in things, and didn't understand that shepherds become attached to their sheep. He knew everything about each member of his flock: he knew which ones were lame, which one was to give birth two months from now, and which were the laziest. He knew how to shear them, and how to slaughter them. If he ever decided to leave them, they would suffer.

The wind began to pick up. He knew that wind: people called it the levanter, because on it the Moors had come from the Levant at the eastern end of the Mediterranean.

The levanter increased in intensity. Here I am, between my flock and my treasure, the boy thought. He had to choose between something he had become accustomed to and something he wanted to have. There was also the merchant's daughter, but she wasn't as important as his flock, because she didn't depend on him. Maybe she didn't even remember him. He was sure that it made no difference to her on which day he appeared: for her, every day was the same, and when each day is the same as the next, it's because people fail to recognize the good things that happen in their lives every day that the sun rises.

I left my father, my mother, and the town castle behind. They have gotten used to my being away, and so have I. The sheep will get used to my not being there, too, the boy thought.

From where he sat, he could observe the plaza. People continued to come and go from the baker's shop. A young couple sat on the bench where he had talked with the old man, and they kissed.

"That baker ...," he said to himself, without completing the thought. The levanter was still getting stronger, and he felt its force on his face. That wind had brought the Moors, yes, but it had also brought the smell of the desert and of veiled women. It had brought with it the sweat and the dreams of men who had once left to search for the unknown, and for gold and adventure— and for the Pyramids. The boy felt jealous of the freedom of the wind, and saw that he could have the same freedom. There was nothing to hold him back except himself. The sheep, the merchant's daughter, and the fields of Andalusia were only steps along the way to his destiny.

The next day, the boy met the old man at noon. He brought six sheep with him.

"I'm surprised," the boy said. "My friend bought all the other sheep immediately. He said that he had always dreamed of being a shepherd, and that it was a good omen."

"That's the way it always is," said the old man. "It's called the principle of favorability. When you play cards the first time, you are almost sure to win. Beginner's luck."

"Why is that?"

"Because there is a force that wants you to realize your destiny; it whets your appetite with a taste of success."

Then the old man began to inspect the sheep, and he saw that one was lame. The boy explained that it wasn't important, since that sheep was the most intelligent of the flock, and produced the most wool.

"Where is the treasure?" he asked.

"It's in Egypt, near the Pyramids."

The boy was startled. The old woman had said the same thing. But she hadn't charged him anything.

"In order to find the treasure, you will have to follow the omens. God has prepared a path for everyone to follow. You just have to read the omens that he left for you."

Before the boy could reply, a butterfly appeared and fluttered between him and the old man. He remembered something his grandfather had once told him: that butterflies were a good omen. Like crickets, and like expectations; like lizards and four-leaf clovers.

"That's right," said the old man, able to read the boy's thoughts. "Just as your grandfather taught you. These are good omens."

The old man opened his cape, and the boy was struck by what he saw. The old man wore a breastplate of heavy gold, covered with precious stones. The boy recalled the brilliance he had noticed on the previous day.

He really was a king! He must be disguised to avoid encounters with thieves.

"Take these," said the old man, holding out a white stone and a black stone that had been embedded at the center of the breastplate. "They are called Urim and Thummim. The black signifies 'yes,' and the white 'no.' When you are unable to read the omens, they will help you to do so. Always ask an objective question.

"But, if you can, try to make your own decisions. The treasure is at the Pyramids; that you already knew.

But I had to insist on the payment of six sheep because I helped you to make your decision."

The boy put the stones in his pouch. From then on, he would make his own decisions.

"Don't forget that everything you deal with is only one thing and nothing else. And don't forget the language of omens. And, above all, don't forget to follow your destiny through to its conclusion.

"But before I go, I want to tell you a little story.

"A certain shopkeeper sent his son to learn about the secret of happiness from the wisest man in the world. The lad wandered through the desert for forty days, and finally came upon a beautiful castle, high atop a mountain. It was there that the wise man lived.

"Rather than finding a saintly man, though, our hero, on entering the main room of the castle, saw a hive of activity: tradesmen came and went, people were conversing in the corners, a small orchestra was playing soft music, and there was a table covered with platters of the most delicious food in that part of the world. The wise man conversed with everyone, and the boy had to wait for two hours before it was his turn to be given the man's attention.

"The wise man listened attentively to the boy's explanation of why he had come, but told him that he didn't have time just then to explain the secret of happiness. He suggested that the boy look around the palace and return in two hours.

"'Meanwhile, I want to ask you to do something,' said the wise man, handing the boy a teaspoon that held two drops of oil. 'As you wander around, carry this spoon with you without allowing the oil to spill.'

"The boy began climbing and descending the many stairways of the palace, keeping his eyes fixed on the spoon. After two hours, he returned to the room where the wise man was.

"'Well,' asked the wise man, 'did you see the Persian tapestries that are hanging in my dining hall? Did you see the garden that it took the master gardener ten years to create? Did you notice the beautiful parchments in my library?'

"The boy was embarrassed, and confessed that he had observed nothing. His only concern had been not to spill the oil that the wise man had entrusted to him.

"'Then go back and observe the marvels of my world,' said the wise man. 'You cannot trust a man if you don't know his house.'

"Relieved, the boy picked up the spoon and returned to his exploration of the palace, this time observing all of the works of art on the ceilings and the walls. He saw the gardens, the mountains all around him, the beauty of the flowers, and the taste with which everything had been selected. Upon returning to the wise man, he related in detail everything he had seen.

"'But where are the drops of oil I entrusted to you?' asked the wise man.

"Looking down at the spoon he held, the boy saw that the oil was gone.

"'Well, there is only one piece of advice I can give you,' said the wisest of wise men. 'The secret of happiness is to see all the marvels of the world, and never to forget the drops of oil on the spoon.'"

The shepherd said nothing. He had understood the story the old king had told him. A shepherd may like to travel, but he should never forget about his sheep.

The old man looked at the boy and, with his hands held together, made several strange gestures over the boy's head. Then, taking his sheep, he walked away.

* * *

At the highest point in Tarifa there is an old fort, built by the Moors. From atop its walls, one can catch a glimpse of Africa. Melchizedek, the king of Salem, sat on the wall of the fort that afternoon, and felt the levanter blowing in his face. The sheep fidgeted nearby, uneasy with their new owner and excited by so much change. All they wanted was food and water.

Melchizedek watched a small ship that was plowing its way out of the port. He would never again see the boy, just as he had never seen Abraham again after having charged him his one-tenth fee. That was his work.

The gods should not have desires, because they don't have destinies. But the king of Salem hoped desperately that the boy would be successful.

It's too bad that he's quickly going to forget my name, he thought. I should have repeated it for him. Then when he spoke about me he would say that I am Melchizedek, the king of Salem.

He looked to the skies, feeling a bit abashed, and said, "I know it's the vanity of vanities, as you said, my Lord. But an old king sometimes has to take some pride in himself."

* * *

How strange Africa is, thought the boy.

He was sitting in a bar very much like the other bars he had seen along the narrow streets of Tangier. Some men were smoking from a gigantic pipe that they passed from one to the other. In just a few hours he had seen men walking hand in hand, women with their faces covered, and priests that climbed to the tops of towers and chanted—as everyone about him went to their knees and placed their foreheads on the ground.

"A practice of infidels," he said to himself. As a child in church, he had always looked at the image of Saint Santiago Matamoros on his white horse, his sword unsheathed, and figures such as these kneeling at his feet. The boy felt ill and terribly alone. The infidels had an evil look about them.

Besides this, in the rush of his travels he had forgotten a detail, just one detail, which could keep him from his treasure for a long time: only Arabic was spoken in this country.

The owner of the bar approached him, and the boy pointed to a drink that had been served at the next table. It turned out to be a bitter tea. The boy preferred wine.

But he didn't need to worry about that right now. What he had to be concerned about was his treasure, and how he was going to go about getting it. The sale of his sheep had left him with enough money in his pouch, and the boy knew that in money there was magic; whoever has money is never really alone. Before long, maybe in just a few days, he would be at the Pyramids. An old man, with a breastplate of gold, wouldn't have lied just to acquire six sheep.

The old man had spoken about signs and omens, and, as the boy was crossing the strait, he had thought about omens. Yes, the old man had known what he was talking about: during the time the boy had spent in the fields of Andalusia, he had become used to learning which path he should take by observing the ground and the sky. He had discovered that the presence of a certain bird meant that a snake was nearby, and that a certain shrub was a sign that there was water in the area. The sheep had taught him that.

If God leads the sheep so well, he will also lead a man, he thought, and that made him feel better. The tea seemed less bitter.

"Who are you?" he heard a voice ask him in Spanish.

The boy was relieved. He was thinking about omens, and someone had appeared.

"How come you speak Spanish?" he asked. The new arrival was a young man in Western dress, but the color of his skin suggested he was from this city. He was about the same age and height as the boy.

"Almost everyone here speaks Spanish. We're only two hours from Spain."

"Sit down, and let me treat you to something," said the boy. "And ask for a glass of wine for me. I hate this tea."

"There is no wine in this country," the young man said. "The religion here forbids it."

The boy told him then that he needed to get to the Pyramids. He almost began to tell about his treasure, but decided not to do so. If he did, it was possible that the Arab would want a part of it as payment for taking him there. He remembered what the old man had said about offering something you didn't even have yet.

"I'd like you to take me there if you can. I can pay you to serve as my guide."

"Do you have any idea how to get there?" the newcomer asked.

The boy noticed that the owner of the bar stood nearby, listening attentively to their conversation. He felt uneasy at the man's presence. But he had found a guide, and didn't want to miss out on an opportunity.

"You have to cross the entire Sahara desert," said the young man. "And to do that, you need money. I need to know whether you have enough."

The boy thought it a strange question. But he trusted in the old man, who had said that, when you really want something, the universe always conspires in your favor.

He took his money from his pouch and showed it to

the young man. The owner of the bar came over and looked, as well. The two men exchanged some words in Arabic, and the bar owner seemed irritated.

"Let's get out of here," said the new arrival. "He wants us to leave."

The boy was relieved. He got up to pay the bill, but the owner grabbed him and began to speak to him in an angry stream of words. The boy was strong, and wanted to retaliate, but he was in a foreign country. His new friend pushed the owner aside, and pulled the boy outside with him. "He wanted your money," he said. "Tangier is not like the rest of Africa. This is a port, and every port has its thieves."

The boy trusted his new friend. He had helped him out in a dangerous situation. He took out his money and counted it.

"We could get to the Pyramids by tomorrow," said the other, taking the money. "But I have to buy two camels."

They walked together through the narrow streets of Tangier. Everywhere there were stalls with items for sale. They reached the center of a large plaza where the market was held. There were thousands of people there, arguing, selling, and buying; vegetables for sale amongst daggers, and carpets displayed alongside tobacco. But the boy never took his eye off his new friend. After all, he had all his money. He thought about asking him to give it back, but decided that would be unfriendly. He knew nothing about the customs of the strange land he was in.

"I'll just watch him," he said to himself. He knew he was stronger than his friend.

Suddenly, there in the midst of all that confusion, he saw the most beautiful sword he had ever seen. The scabbard was embossed in silver, and the handle was black and encrusted with precious stones. The boy promised himself that, when he returned from Egypt, he would buy that sword.

"Ask the owner of that stall how much the sword costs," he said to his friend. Then he realized that he had been distracted for a few moments, looking at the sword. His heart squeezed, as if his chest had suddenly compressed it. He was afraid to look around, because he knew what he would find. He continued to look at the beautiful sword for a bit longer, until he summoned the courage to turn around.

All around him was the market, with people coming and going, shouting and buying, and the aroma of strange foods ... but nowhere could he find his new companion.

The boy wanted to believe that his friend had simply become separated from him by accident. He decided to stay right there and await his return. As he waited, a priest climbed to the top of a nearby tower and began his chant; everyone in the market fell to their knees, touched their foreheads to the ground, and took up the chant. Then, like a colony of worker ants, they dismantled their stalls and left.

The sun began its departure, as well. The boy watched it through its trajectory for some time, until it was hidden behind the white houses surrounding the plaza. He recalled that when the sun had risen that morning, he was on another continent, still a shepherd with sixty sheep, and looking forward to meeting with a girl. That morning he had known everything that was going to happen to him as he walked through the familiar fields. But now, as the sun began to set, he was in a different country, a stranger in a strange land, where he couldn't even speak the language. He was no longer a shepherd, and he had nothing, not even the money to return and start everything over.

All this happened between sunrise and sunset, the boy thought. He was feeling sorry for himself, and lamenting the fact that his life could have changed so suddenly and so drastically.

He was so ashamed that he wanted to cry. He had never even wept in front of his own sheep. But the marketplace was empty, and he was far from home, so he wept. He wept because God was unfair, and because this was the way God repaid those who believed in their dreams.

When I had my sheep, I was happy, and I made those around me happy. People saw me coming and welcomed me, he thought. But now I'm sad and alone. I'm going to become bitter and distrustful of people because one person betrayed me. I'm going to hate those who have found their treasure because I never found mine. And I'm going to hold on to what little I have, because I'm too insignificant to conquer the world.

He opened his pouch to see what was left of his possessions; maybe there was a bit left of the sandwich he had eaten on the ship. But all he found was the heavy book, his jacket, and the two stones the old man had given him.

As he looked at the stones, he felt relieved for some reason. He had exchanged six sheep for two precious stones that had been taken from a gold breastplate. He could sell the stones and buy a return ticket. But this time I'll be smarter, the boy thought, removing them from the pouch so he could put them in his pocket. This was a port town, and the only truthful thing his friend had told him was that port towns are full of thieves.

Now he understood why the owner of the bar had been so upset: he was trying to tell him not to trust that man. "I'm like everyone else—I see the world in terms of what I would like to see happen, not what actually does."

He ran his fingers slowly over the stones, sensing their temperature and feeling their surfaces. They were his treasure. Just handling them made him feel better. They reminded him of the old man.

"When you want something, all the universe conspires in helping you to achieve it," he had said.

The boy was trying to understand the truth of what the old man had said. There he was in the empty marketplace, without a cent to his name, and with not a sheep to guard through the night. But the stones were proof that he had met with a king—a king who knew of the boy's past.

"They're called Urim and Thummim, and they can help you to read the omens." The boy put the stones back in the pouch and decided to do an experiment. The old man had said to ask very clear questions, and to do that, the boy had to know what he wanted. So, he asked if the old man's blessing was still with him.

He took out one of the stones. It was "yes."

"Am I going to find my treasure?" he asked. He stuck his hand into the pouch, and felt around for one of the stones. As he did so, both of them pushed through a hole in the pouch and fell to the ground. The boy had never even noticed that there was a hole in his pouch. He knelt down to find Urim and Thummim and put them back in the pouch. But as he saw them lying there on the ground, another phrase came to his mind.

"Learn to recognize omens, and follow them," the old king had said.

An omen. The boy smiled to himself. He picked up the two stones and put them back in his pouch. He didn't consider mending the hole—the stones could fall through any time they wanted. He had learned that there were certain things one shouldn't ask about, so as not to flee from one's own destiny. "I promised that I would make my own decisions," he said to himself.

But the stones had told him that the old man was still with him, and that made him feel more confident. He looked around at the empty plaza again, feeling less desperate than before. This wasn't a strange place; it was a new one.

After all, what he had always wanted was just that: to know new places. Even if he never got to the Pyramids, he had already traveled farther than any shepherd he knew. Oh, if they only knew how different things are just two hours by ship from where they are, he thought. Although his new world at the moment was just an empty marketplace, he had already seen it when it was teeming with life, and he would never forget it. He remembered the sword. It hurt him a bit to think about it, but he had never seen one like it before. As he mused about these things, he realized that he had to choose between thinking of himself as the poor victim of a thief and as an adventurer in quest of his treasure.

"I'm an adventurer, looking for treasure," he said to himself.

* * *

He was shaken into wakefulness by someone. He had fallen asleep in the middle of the marketplace, and life in the plaza was about to resume. Looking around, he sought his sheep, and then realized that he was in a new world. But instead of being saddened, he was happy. He no longer had to seek out food and water for the sheep; he could go in search of his treasure, instead. He had not a cent in his pocket, but he had faith. He had decided, the night before, that he would be as much an adventurer as the ones he had admired in books.

He walked slowly through the market. The merchants were assembling their stalls, and the boy helped a candy seller to do his. The candy seller had a smile on his face: he was happy, aware of what his life was about, and ready to begin a day's work. His smile reminded the boy of the old man—the mysterious old king he had met. "This candy merchant isn't making candy so that later he can travel or marry a shopkeeper's daughter. He's doing it because it's what he wants to do," thought the boy. He realized that he could do the same thing the old man had done—sense whether a person was near to or far from his destiny. Just by looking at them. It's easy, and yet I've never done it before, he thought.

When the stall was assembled, the candy seller offered the boy the first sweet he had made for the day. The boy thanked him, ate it, and went on his way. When he had gone only a short distance, he realized that, while they were erecting the stall, one of them had spoken Arabic and the other Spanish.

And they had understood each other perfectly well.

There must be a language that doesn't depend on words, the boy thought. I've already had that experience with my sheep, and now it's happening with people.

He was learning a lot of new things. Some of them were things that he had already experienced, and weren't really new, but that he had never perceived before. And he hadn't perceived them because he had become accustomed to them. He realized: If I can learn to understand this language without words, I can learn to understand the world.

Relaxed and unhurried, he resolved that he would walk through the narrow streets of Tangier. Only in that way would he be able to read the omens. He knew it would require a lot of patience, but shepherds know all about patience. Once again he saw that, in that strange land, he was applying the same lessons he had learned with his sheep.

"All things are one," the old man had said.

* * *

The crystal merchant awoke with the day, and felt the same anxiety that he felt every morning. He had been in the same place for thirty years: a shop at the top of a hilly street where few customers passed. Now it was too late to change anything—the only thing he had ever learned to do was to buy and sell crystal glassware. There had been a time when many people knew of his shop: Arab merchants, French and English geologists, German soldiers who were always well-heeled. In those days it had been wonderful to be selling crystal, and he had thought how he would become rich, and have beautiful women at his side as he grew older.

But, as time passed, Tangier had changed. The nearby city of Ceuta had grown faster than Tangier, and business had fallen off. Neighbors moved away, and there remained only a few small shops on the hill. And no one was going to climb the hill just to browse through a few small shops.

But the crystal merchant had no choice. He had lived thirty years of his life buying and selling crystal pieces, and now it was too late to do anything else.

He spent the entire morning observing the infrequent comings and goings in the street. He had done this for years, and knew the schedule of everyone who passed. But, just before lunchtime, a boy stopped in front of the shop. He was dressed normally, but the practiced eyes of the crystal merchant could see that the boy had no money to spend. Nevertheless, the merchant decided to delay his lunch for a few minutes until the boy moved on.

* * *

A card hanging in the doorway announced that several languages were spoken in the shop. The boy saw a man appear behind the counter.

"I can clean up those glasses in the window, if you want," said the boy. "The way they look now, nobody is going to want to buy them."

The man looked at him without responding.

"In exchange, you could give me something to eat."

The man still said nothing, and the boy sensed that he was going to have to make a decision. In his pouch, he had his jacket—he certainly wasn't going to need it in the desert. Taking the jacket out, he began to clean the glasses. In half an hour, he had cleaned all the glasses in the window, and, as he was doing so, two customers had entered the shop and bought some crystal.

When he had completed the cleaning, he asked the man for something to eat. "Let's go and have some lunch," said the crystal merchant.

He put a sign on the door, and they went to a small cafe nearby. As they sat down at the only table in the place, the crystal merchant laughed.

"You didn't have to do any cleaning," he said. "The Koran requires me to feed a hungry person."

"Well then, why did you let me do it?" the boy asked.

"Because the crystal was dirty. And both you and I needed to cleanse our minds of negative thoughts."

When they had eaten, the merchant turned to the boy and said, "I'd like you to work in my shop. Two customers came in today while you were working, and that's a good omen."

People talk a lot about omens, thought the shepherd. But they really don't know what they're saying. Just as I hadn't realized that for so many years I had been speaking a language without words to my sheep.

"Do you want to go to work for me?" the merchant asked.

"I can work for the rest of today," the boy answered. "I'll work all night, until dawn, and I'll clean every piece of crystal in your shop. In return, I need money to get to Egypt tomorrow."

The merchant laughed. "Even if you cleaned my crystal for an entire year ... even if you earned a good commission selling every piece, you would still have to borrow money to get to Egypt. There are thousands of kilometers of desert between here and there."

There was a moment of silence so profound that it seemed the city was asleep. No sound from the bazaars, no arguments among the merchants, no men climbing to the towers to chant. No hope, no adventure, no old kings or destinies, no treasure, and no Pyramids. It was as if the world had fallen silent because the boy's soul had. He sat there, staring blankly through the door of the cafe, wishing that he had died, and that everything would end forever at that moment.

The merchant looked anxiously at the boy. All the joy he had seen that morning had suddenly disappeared.

"I can give you the money you need to get back to your country, my son," said the crystal merchant.

The boy said nothing. He got up, adjusted his clothing, and picked up his pouch.

"I'll work for you," he said.

And after another long silence, he added, "I need money to buy some sheep."

Part Two

The boy had been working for the crystal merchant for almost a month, and he could see that it wasn't exactly the kind of job that would make him happy. The merchant spent the entire day mumbling behind the counter, telling the boy to be careful with the pieces and not to break anything.

But he stayed with the job because the merchant, although he was an old grouch, treated him fairly; the boy received a good commission for each piece he sold, and had already been able to put some money aside. That morning he had done some calculating: if he continued to work every day as he had been, he would need a whole year to be able to buy some sheep.

"I'd like to build a display case for the crystal," the boy said to the merchant. "We could place it outside, and attract those people who pass at the bottom of the hill."

"I've never had one before," the merchant answered. "People will pass by and bump into it, and pieces will be broken."

"Well, when I took my sheep through the fields some of them might have died if we had come upon a snake. But that's the way life is with sheep and with shepherds."

The merchant turned to a customer who wanted three crystal glasses. He was selling better than ever … as if time had turned back to the old days when the street had been one of Tangier's major attractions.

"Business has really improved," he said to the boy, after the customer had left. "I'm doing much better, and soon you'll be able to return to your sheep. Why ask more out of life?"

"Because we have to respond to omens," the boy said, almost without meaning to; then he regretted what he had said, because the merchant had never met the king.

"It's called the principle of favorability, beginner's luck. Because life wants you to achieve your destiny," the old king had said.

But the merchant understood what the boy had said. The boy's very presence in the shop was an omen, and, as time passed and money was pouring into the cash drawer, he had no regrets about having hired the boy. The boy was being paid more money than he deserved, because the merchant, thinking that sales wouldn't amount to much, had offered the boy a high commission rate. He had assumed he would soon return to his sheep.

"Why did you want to get to the Pyramids?" he asked, to get away from the business of the display.

"Because I've always heard about them," the boy answered, saying nothing about his dream. The treasure was now nothing but a painful memory, and he tried to avoid thinking about it.

"I don't know anyone around here who would want to cross the desert just to see the Pyramids," said the merchant. "They're just a pile of stones. You could build one in your backyard."

"You've never had dreams of travel," said the boy, turning to wait on a customer who had entered the shop.

Two days later, the merchant spoke to the boy about the display.

"I don't much like change," he said. "You and I aren't like Hassan, that rich merchant. If he makes a buying mistake, it doesn't affect him much. But we two have to live with our mistakes."

That's true enough, the boy thought, ruefully.

"Why did you think we should have the display?"

"I want to get back to my sheep faster. We have to take advantage when luck is on our side, and do as much to help it as it's doing to help us. It's called the principle of favorability. Or beginner's luck."

The merchant was silent for a few moments. Then he said, "The Prophet gave us the Koran, and left us just five obligations to satisfy during our lives. The most important is to believe only in the one true God. The others are to pray five times a day, fast during Ramadan, and be charitable to the poor."

He stopped there. His eyes filled with tears as he spoke of the Prophet. He was a devout man, and, even with all his impatience, he wanted to live his life in accordance with Muslim law.

"What's the fifth obligation?" the boy asked.

"Two days ago, you said that I had never dreamed

of travel," the merchant answered. "The fifth obligation of every Muslim is a pilgrimage. We are obliged, at least once in our lives, to visit the holy city of Mecca.

"Mecca is a lot farther away than the Pyramids. When I was young, all I wanted to do was put together enough money to start this shop. I thought that someday I'd be rich, and could go to Mecca. I began to make some money, but I could never bring myself to leave someone in charge of the shop; the crystals are delicate things. At the same time, people were passing my shop all the time, heading for Mecca. Some of them were rich pilgrims, traveling in caravans with servants and camels, but most of the people making the pilgrimage were poorer than I.

"All who went there were happy at having done so. They placed the symbols of the pilgrimage on the doors of their houses. One of them, a cobbler who made his living mending boots, said that he had traveled for almost a year through the desert, but that he got more tired when he had to walk through the streets of Tangier buying his leather."

"Well, why don't you go to Mecca now?" asked the boy.

"Because it's the thought of Mecca that keeps me alive. That's what helps me face these days that are all the same, these mute crystals on the shelves, and lunch and dinner at that same horrible cafe. I'm afraid that if my dream is realized, I'll have no reason to go on living.

"You dream about your sheep and the Pyramids, but you're different from me, because you want to realize your dreams. I just want to dream about Mecca. I've already imagined a thousand times crossing the desert, arriving at the Plaza of the Sacred Stone, the seven times I walk around it before allowing myself to touch it. I've already imagined the people who would be at my side, and those in front of me, and the conversations and prayers we would share. But I'm afraid that it would all be a disappointment, so I prefer just to dream about it."

That day, the merchant gave the boy permission to build the display. Not everyone can see his dreams come true in the same way.

* * *

Two more months passed, and the shelf brought many customers into the crystal shop. The boy estimated that, if he worked for six more months, he could return to Spain and buy sixty sheep, and yet another sixty. In less than a year, he would have doubled his flock, and he would be able to do business with the Arabs, because he was now able to speak their strange language. Since that morning in the marketplace, he had never again made use of Urim and Thummim, because Egypt was now just as distant a dream for him as was Mecca for the merchant. Anyway, the boy had become happy in his work, and thought all the time about the day when he would disembark at Tarifa as a winner.

"You must always know what it is that you want," the old king had said. The boy knew, and was now working toward it. Maybe it was his treasure to have wound up in that strange land, met up with a thief, and doubled the size of his flock without spending a cent.

He was proud of himself. He had learned some important things, like how to deal in crystal, and about the language without words ... and about omens. One afternoon he had seen a man at the top of the hill, complaining that it was impossible to find a decent place to get something to drink after such a climb. The boy, accustomed to recognizing omens, spoke to the merchant.

"Let's sell tea to the people who climb the hill."

"Lots of places sell tea around here," the merchant said.

"But we could sell tea in crystal glasses. The people will enjoy the tea and want to buy the glasses. I have been told that beauty is the great seducer of men."

The merchant didn't respond, but that afternoon, after saying his prayers and closing the shop, he invited the boy to sit with him and share his hookah, that strange pipe used by the Arabs.

"What is it you're looking for?" asked the old merchant.

"I've already told you. I need to buy my sheep back, so I have to earn the money to do so."

The merchant put some new coals in the hookah, and inhaled deeply.

"I've had this shop for thirty years. I know good crystal from bad, and everything else there is to know about crystal. I know its dimensions and how it behaves. If we serve tea in crystal, the shop is going to expand. And then I'll have to change my way of life."

"Well, isn't that good?"

"I'm already used to the way things are. Before you came, I was thinking about how much time I had wasted in the same place, while my friends had moved on, and either went bankrupt or did better than they had before. It made me very depressed. Now, I can see that it hasn't been too bad. The shop is exactly the size I always wanted it to be. I don't want to change anything, because I don't know how to deal with change. I'm used to the way I am."

The boy didn't know what to say. The old man continued, "You have been a real blessing to me. Today, I understand something I didn't see before: every blessing ignored becomes a curse. I don't want anything else in life. But you are forcing me to look at wealth and at horizons I have never known. Now that I have seen them, and now that I see how immense my possibilities are, I'm going to feel worse than I did before you arrived. Because I know the things I should be able to accomplish, and I don't want to do so."

It's good I refrained from saying anything to the baker in Tarifa, thought the boy to himself.

They went on smoking the pipe for a while as the sun began to set. They were conversing in Arabic, and the boy was proud of himself for being able to do so. There had been a time when he thought that his sheep could teach him everything he needed to know about the world. But they could never have taught him Arabic.

There are probably other things in the world that the sheep can't teach me, thought the boy as he regarded the old merchant. All they ever do, really, is look for food and water. And maybe it wasn't that they were teaching me, but that I was learning from them.

"Maktub," the merchant said, finally.

"What does that mean?"

"You would have to have been born an Arab to understand," he answered. "But in your language it would be something like 'It is written.'"

And, as he smothered the coals in the hookah, he told the boy that he could begin to sell tea in the crystal glasses. Sometimes, there's just no way to hold back the river.

* * *

The men climbed the hill, and they were tired when they reached the top. But there they saw a crystal shop that offered refreshing mint tea. They went in to drink the tea, which was served in beautiful crystal glasses.

"My wife never thought of this," said one, and he bought some crystal—he was entertaining guests that night, and the guests would be impressed by the beauty of the glassware. The other man remarked that tea was always more delicious when it was served in crystal, because the aroma was retained. The third said that it was a tradition in the Orient to use crystal glasses for tea because it had magical powers.

Before long, the news spread, and a great many people began to climb the hill to see the shop that was doing something new in a trade that was so old. Other shops were opened that served tea in crystal, but they weren't at the top of a hill, and they had little business.

Eventually, the merchant had to hire two more employees. He began to import enormous quantities of tea, along with his crystal, and his shop was sought out by men and women with a thirst for things new.

And, in that way, the months passed.

* * *

The boy awoke before dawn. It had been eleven months and nine days since he had first set foot on the African continent.

He dressed in his Arabian clothing of white linen, bought especially for this day. He put his headcloth in place and secured it with a ring made of camel skin. Wearing his new sandals, he descended the stairs silently.

The city was still sleeping. He prepared himself a sandwich and drank some hot tea from a crystal glass. Then he sat in the sun-filled doorway, smoking the hookah.

He smoked in silence, thinking of nothing, and listening to the sound of the wind that brought the scent of the desert. When he had finished his smoke, he reached into one of his pockets, and sat there for a few moments, regarding what he had withdrawn.

It was a bundle of money. Enough to buy himself a hundred and twenty sheep, a return ticket, and a license to import products from Africa into his own country.

He waited patiently for the merchant to awaken and open the shop. Then the two went off to have some more tea.

"I'm leaving today," said the boy. "I have the money I need to buy my sheep. And you have the money you need to go to Mecca."

The old man said nothing.

"Will you give me your blessing?" asked the boy. "You have helped me." The man continued to prepare his tea, saying nothing. Then he turned to the boy.

"I am proud of you," he said. "You brought a new feeling into my crystal shop. But you know that I'm not going to go to Mecca. Just as you know that you're not going to buy your sheep."

"Who told you that?" asked the boy, startled.

"Maktub," said the old crystal merchant.

And he gave the boy his blessing.

* * *

The boy went to his room and packed his belongings. They filled three sacks. As he was leaving, he saw, in the corner of the room, his old shepherd's pouch.

It was bunched up, and he had hardly thought of it for a long time. As he took his jacket out of the pouch, thinking to give it to someone in the street, the two stones fell to the floor. Urim and Thummim.

It made the boy think of the old king, and it startled him to realize how long it had been since he had thought of him. For nearly a year, he had been working incessantly, thinking only of putting aside enough money so that he could return to Spain with pride.

"Never stop dreaming," the old king had said. "Follow the omens."

The boy picked up Urim and Thummim, and, once again, had the strange sensation that the old king was nearby. He had worked hard for a year, and the omens were that it was time to go.

I'm going to go back to doing just what I did before, the boy thought. Even though the sheep didn't teach me to speak Arabic.

But the sheep had taught him something even more important; that there was a language in the world that everyone understood, a language the boy had used throughout the time that he was trying to improve things at the shop. It was the language of enthusiasm, of things accomplished with love and purpose, and as part of a search for something believed in and desired. Tangier was no longer a strange city, and he felt that, just as he had conquered this place, he could conquer the world.

"When you want something, all the universe conspires to help you achieve it," the old king had said.

But the old king hadn't said anything about being robbed, or about endless deserts, or about people who know what their dreams are but don't want to realize them. The old king hadn't told him that the Pyramids were just a pile of stones, or that anyone could build one in his backyard. And he had forgotten to mention that, when you have enough money to buy a flock larger than the one you had before, you should buy it.

The boy picked up his pouch and put it with his other things. He went down the stairs and found the merchant waiting on a foreign couple, while two other customers walked about the shop, drinking tea from crystal glasses. It was more activity than usual for this time of the morning. From where he stood, he saw for the first time that the old merchant's hair was very much like the hair of the old king. He remembered the smile of the candy seller, on his first day in Tangier, when he had nothing to eat and nowhere to go — that smile had also been like the old king's smile.

It's almost as if he had been here and left his mark, he thought. And yet, none of these people has ever met the old king. On the other hand, he said that he always appeared to help those who are trying to realize their destiny.

He left without saying good-bye to the crystal merchant. He didn't want to cry with the other people there. He was going to miss the place and all the good things he had learned. He was more confident in himself, though, and felt as though he could conquer the world.

"But I'm going back to the fields that I know, to take care of my flock again." He said that to himself with certainty, but he was no longer happy with his decision. He had worked for an entire year to make a dream come true, and that dream, minute by minute, was becoming less important. Maybe because that wasn't really his dream.

Who knows … maybe it's better to be like the crystal merchant: never go to Mecca, and just go through life wanting to do so, he thought, again trying to convince himself. But as he held Urim and Thummim in his hand, they had transmitted to him the strength and will of the old king. By coincidence — or maybe it was an omen, the boy thought — he came to the bar he had entered on his first day there. The thief wasn't there, and the owner brought him a cup of tea.

I can always go back to being a shepherd, the boy thought. I learned how to care for sheep, and I haven't forgotten how that's done. But maybe I'll never have another chance to get to the Pyramids in Egypt. The old man wore a breastplate of gold, and he knew about my past. He really was a king, a wise king.

The hills of Andalusia were only two hours away, but there was an entire desert between him and the Pyramids. Yet the boy felt that there was another way to regard his situation: he was actually two hours closer to his treasure … the fact that the two hours had stretched into an entire year didn't matter.

I know why I want to get back to my flock, he thought. I understand sheep; they're no longer a problem, and they can be good friends. On the other hand, I don't know if the desert can be a friend, and it's in the desert that I have to search for my treasure. If I don't find it, I can always go home. I finally have enough money, and all the time I need. Why not?

He suddenly felt tremendously happy. He could always go back to being a shepherd. He could always become a crystal salesman again. Maybe the world had other hidden treasures, but he had a dream, and he had met with a king. That doesn't happen to just anyone!

He was planning as he left the bar. He had remembered that one of the crystal merchant's suppliers transported his crystal by means of caravans that crossed the desert. He held Urim and Thummim in his hand; because of those two stones, he was once again on the way to his treasure.

"I am always nearby, when someone wants to realize their destiny," the old king had told him.

What could it cost to go over to the supplier's warehouse and find out if the Pyramids were really that far away?

* * *

The Englishman was sitting on a bench in a structure that smelled of animals, sweat, and dust; it was part warehouse, part corral. I never thought I'd end up in a place like this, he thought, as he leafed through the pages of a chemical journal. Ten years at the university, and here I am in a corral.

But he had to move on. He believed in omens. All his life and all his studies were aimed at finding the one true language of the universe. First he had studied Esperanto, then the world's religions, and now it was alchemy. He knew how to speak Esperanto, he understood all the major religions well, but he wasn't yet an alchemist. He had unraveled the truths behind important questions, but his studies had taken him to a point beyond which he could not seem to go. He had tried in vain to establish a relationship with an alchemist. But the alchemists were strange people, who thought only about themselves, and almost always refused to help him. Who knows, maybe they had failed to discover the secret of the Master Work—the Philosopher's Stone—and for this reason kept their knowledge to themselves.

He had already spent much of the fortune left to him by his father, fruitlessly seeking the Philosopher's Stone. He had spent enormous amounts of time at the great libraries of the world, and had purchased all the rarest and most important volumes on alchemy. In one he had read that, many years ago, a famous Arabian alchemist had visited Europe. It was said that he was more than two hundred years old, and that he had discovered the Philosopher's Stone and the Elixir of Life. The Englishman had been profoundly impressed by the story. But he would never have thought it more than just a myth, had not a friend of his—returning from an archaeological expedition in the desert—told him about an Arab that was possessed of exceptional powers.

"He lives at the Al-Fayoum oasis," his friend had said. "And people say that he is two hundred years old, and is able to transform any metal into gold."

The Englishman could not contain his excitement. He canceled all his commitments and pulled together the most important of his books, and now here he was, sitting inside a dusty, smelly warehouse. Outside, a huge caravan was being prepared for a crossing of the Sahara, and was scheduled to pass through Al-Fayoum.

I'm going to find that damned alchemist, the Englishman thought. And the odor of the animals became a bit more tolerable.

A young Arab, also loaded down with baggage, entered, and greeted the Englishman.

"Where are you bound?" asked the young Arab.

"I'm going into the desert," the man answered, turning back to his reading. He didn't want any conversation at this point. What he needed to do was review all he had learned over the years, because the alchemist would certainly put him to the test.

The young Arab took out a book and began to read. The book was written in Spanish. That's good, thought the Englishman. He spoke Spanish better than Arabic, and, if this boy was going to Al-Fayoum, there would be someone to talk to when there were no other important things to do.

* * *

"That's strange," said the boy, as he tried once again to read the burial scene that began the book. "I've been trying for two years to read this book, and I never get past these first few pages." Even without a king to provide an interruption, he was unable to concentrate.

He still had some doubts about the decision he had made. But he was able to understand one thing: making a decision was only the beginning of things. When someone makes a decision, he is really diving into a strong current that will carry him to places he had never dreamed of when he first made the decision.

When I decided to seek out my treasure, I never imagined that I'd wind up working in a crystal shop, he thought. And joining this caravan may have been my decision, but where it goes is going to be a mystery to me.

Nearby was the Englishman, reading a book. He seemed unfriendly, and had looked irritated when the boy had entered. They might even have become friends, but the Englishman closed off the conversation.

The boy closed his book. He felt that he didn't want to do anything that might make him look like the Englishman. He took Urim and Thummim from his pocket, and began playing with them.

The stranger shouted, "Urim and Thummim!"

In a flash the boy put them back in his pocket.

"They're not for sale," he said.

"They're not worth much," the Englishman answered. "They're only made of rock crystal, and there are millions of rock crystals in the earth. But those who know about such things would know that those are Urim and Thummim. I didn't know that they had them in this part of the world."

"They were given to me as a present by a king," the boy said.

The stranger didn't answer; instead, he put his hand in his pocket, and took out two stones that were the same as the boy's.

"Did you say a king?" he asked.

"I guess you don't believe that a king would talk to someone like me, a shepherd," he said, wanting to end the conversation.

"Not at all. It was shepherds who were the first to recognize a king that the rest of the world refused to acknowledge. So, it's not surprising that kings would talk to shepherds."

And he went on, fearing that the boy wouldn't understand what he was talking about, "It's in the Bible. The same book that taught me about Urim and Thummim. These stones were the only form of divination permitted by God. The priests carried them in a golden breastplate."

The boy was suddenly happy to be there at the warehouse.

"Maybe this is an omen," said the Englishman, half aloud.

"Who told you about omens?" The boy's interest was increasing by the moment.

"Everything in life is an omen," said the Englishman,

now closing the journal he was reading. "There is a universal language, understood by everybody, but already forgotten. I am in search of that universal language, among other things. That's why I'm here. I have to find a man who knows that universal language. An alchemist."

The conversation was interrupted by the warehouse boss.

"You're in luck, you two," the fat Arab said. "There's a caravan leaving today for Al-Fayoum."

"But I'm going to Egypt," the boy said.

"Al-Fayoum is in Egypt," said the Arab. "What kind of Arab are you?"

"That's a good luck omen," the Englishman said, after the fat Arab had gone out. "If I could, I'd write a huge encyclopedia just about the words *luck* and *coincidence*. It's with those words that the universal language is written."

He told the boy it was no coincidence that he had met him with Urim and Thummim in his hand. And he asked the boy if he, too, were in search of the alchemist.

"I'm looking for a treasure," said the boy, and he immediately regretted having said it. But the Englishman appeared not to attach any importance to it.

"In a way, so am I," he said.

"I don't even know what alchemy is," the boy was saying, when the warehouse boss called to them to come outside.

* * *

"I'm the leader of the caravan," said a dark-eyed, bearded man. "I hold the power of life and death for every person I take with me. The desert is a capricious lady, and sometimes she drives men crazy."

There were almost two hundred people gathered there, and four hundred animals—camels, horses, mules, and fowl. In the crowd were women, children, and a number of men with swords at their belts and rifles slung on their shoulders. The Englishman had several suitcases filled with books. There was a babble of noise, and the leader had to repeat himself several times for everyone to understand what he was saying.

"There are a lot of different people here, and each has his own God. But the only God I serve is Allah, and in his name I swear that I will do everything possible once again to win out over the desert. But I want each and every one of you to swear by the God you believe in that you will follow my orders no matter what. In the desert, disobedience means death."

There was a murmur from the crowd. Each was swearing quietly to his or her own God. The boy swore to Jesus Christ. The Englishman said nothing. And the murmur lasted longer than a simple vow would have. The people were also praying to heaven for protection.

A long note was sounded on a bugle, and everyone mounted up. The boy and the Englishman had bought camels, and climbed uncertainly onto their backs. The boy felt sorry for the Englishman's camel, loaded down as he was with the cases of books.

"There's no such thing as coincidence," said the Englishman, picking up the conversation where it had been interrupted in the warehouse. "I'm here because a friend of mine heard of an Arab who ..."

But the caravan began to move, and it was impossible to hear what the Englishman was saying. The boy knew what he was about to describe, though: the mysterious chain that links one thing to another, the same chain that had caused him to become a shepherd, that had caused his recurring dream, that had brought him to a city near Africa, to find a king, and to be robbed in order to meet a crystal merchant, and ...

The closer one gets to realizing his destiny, the more that destiny becomes his true reason for being, thought the boy.

The caravan moved toward the east. It traveled during the morning, halted when the sun was at its strongest, and resumed late in the afternoon. The boy spoke very little with the Englishman, who spent most of his time with his books.

The boy observed in silence the progress of the animals and people across the desert. Now everything was quite different from how it was that day they had set out: then, there had been confusion and shouting, the cries of children and the whinnying of animals, all mixed with the nervous orders of the guides and the merchants.

But, in the desert, there was only the sound of the

eternal wind, and of the hoofbeats of the animals. Even the guides spoke very little to one another.

"I've crossed these sands many times," said one of the camel drivers one night. "But the desert is so huge, and the horizons so distant, that they make a person feel small, and as if he should remain silent."

The boy understood intuitively what he meant, even without ever having set foot in the desert before. Whenever he saw the sea, or a fire, he fell silent, impressed by their elemental force.

I've learned things from the sheep, and I've learned things from crystal, he thought. I can learn something from the desert, too. It seems old and wise.

The wind never stopped, and the boy remembered the day he had sat at the fort in Tarifa with this same wind blowing in his face. It reminded him of the wool from his sheep … his sheep who were now seeking food and water in the fields of Andalusia, as they always had.

"They're not my sheep anymore," he said to himself, without nostalgia. "They must be used to their new shepherd, and have probably already forgotten me. That's good. Creatures like the sheep, that are used to traveling, know about moving on."

He thought of the merchant's daughter, and was sure that she had probably married. Perhaps to a baker, or to another shepherd who could read and could tell her exciting stories—after all, he probably wasn't the only one. But he was excited at his intuitive understanding of the camel driver's comment: maybe he was also learning the universal language that deals with the past and the present of all people. "Hunches," his mother used to call them. The boy was beginning to understand that intuition is really a sudden immersion of the soul into the universal current of life, where the histories of all people are connected, and we are able to know everything, because it's all written there.

"*Maktub*," the boy said, remembering the crystal merchant.

The desert was all sand in some stretches, and rocky in others. When the caravan was blocked by a boulder, it had to go around it; if there was a large rocky area, they had to make a major detour. If the sand was too fine for the animals' hooves, they sought a way where the sand was more substantial. In some places, the ground was covered with the salt of dried-up lakes. The animals balked at such places, and the camel drivers were forced to dismount and unburden their charges. The drivers carried the freight themselves over such treacherous footing, and then reloaded the camels. If a guide were to fall ill or die, the camel drivers would draw lots and appoint a new one.

But all this happened for one basic reason: no matter how many detours and adjustments it made, the caravan moved toward the same compass point. Once obstacles were overcome, it returned to its course, sighting on a star that indicated the location of the oasis. When the people saw that star shining in the morning sky, they knew they were on the right course toward water, palm trees, shelter, and other people.

It was only the Englishman who was unaware of all this; he was, for the most part, immersed in reading his books.

The boy, too, had his book, and he had tried to read it during the first few days of the journey. But he found it much more interesting to observe the caravan and listen to the wind. As soon as he had learned to know his camel better, and to establish a relationship with him, he threw the book away. Although the boy had developed a superstition that each time he opened the book he would learn something important, he decided it was an unnecessary burden.

He became friendly with the camel driver who traveled alongside him. At night, as they sat around the fire, the boy related to the driver his adventures as a shepherd.

During one of these conversations, the driver told of his own life.

"I used to live near El Cairum," he said. "I had my orchard, my children, and a life that would change not at all until I died. One year, when the crop was the best ever, we all went to Mecca, and I satisfied the only unmet obligation in my life. I could die happily, and that made me feel good.

"One day, the earth began to tremble, and the Nile overflowed its banks. It was something that I thought could happen only to others, never to me. My neighbors feared they would lose all their olive trees in the flood, and my wife was afraid that we would lose our children. I thought that everything I owned would be destroyed.

"The land was ruined, and I had to find some other way to earn a living. So now I'm a camel driver. But that disaster taught me to understand the word of Allah: people need not fear the unknown if they are capable of achieving what they need and want.

"We are afraid of losing what we have, whether it's our life or our possessions and property. But this fear evaporates when we understand that our life stories and the history of the world were written by the same hand."

Sometimes, their caravan met with another. One always had something that the other needed—as if everything were indeed written by one hand. As they sat around the fire, the camel drivers exchanged information about windstorms, and told stories about the desert.

At other times, mysterious, hooded men would appear; they were Bedouins who did surveillance along the caravan route. They provided warnings about thieves and barbarian tribes. They came in silence and departed the same way, dressed in black garments that showed only their eyes. One night, a camel driver came to the fire where the Englishman and the boy were sitting. "There are rumors of tribal wars," he told them.

The three fell silent. The boy noted that there was a sense of fear in the air, even though no one said anything. Once again he was experiencing the language without words … the universal language.

The Englishman asked if they were in danger.

"Once you get into the desert, there's no going back," said the camel driver. "And, when you can't go back, you have to worry only about the best way of moving forward. The rest is up to Allah, including the danger."

And he concluded by saying the mysterious word: "*Maktub*."

"You should pay more attention to the caravan," the boy said to the Englishman, after the camel driver had left. "We make a lot of detours, but we're always heading for the same destination."

"And you ought to read more about the world," answered the Englishman. "Books are like caravans in that respect."

The immense collection of people and animals began to travel faster. The days had always been silent, but now, even the nights — when the travelers were accustomed to talking around the fires — had also become quiet. And, one day, the leader of the caravan made the decision that the fires should no longer be lighted, so as not to attract attention to the caravan.

The travelers adopted the practice of arranging the animals in a circle at night, sleeping together in the center as protection against the nocturnal cold. And the leader posted armed sentinels at the fringes of the group.

The Englishman was unable to sleep one night. He called to the boy, and they took a walk along the dunes surrounding the encampment. There was a full moon, and the boy told the Englishman the story of his life.

The Englishman was fascinated with the part about the progress achieved at the crystal shop after the boy began working there.

"That's the principle that governs all things," he said. "In alchemy, it's called the Soul of the World. When you want something with all your heart, that's when you are closest to the Soul of the World. It's always a positive force."

He also said that this was not just a human gift, that everything on the face of the earth had a soul, whether mineral, vegetable, or animal — or even just a simple thought.

"Everything on earth is being continuously transformed, because the earth is alive … and it has a soul. We are part of that soul, so we rarely recognize that it is working for us. But in the crystal shop you probably realized that even the glasses were collaborating in your success."

The boy thought about that for a while as he looked at the moon and the bleached sands. "I have watched the caravan as it crossed the desert," he said. "The caravan and the desert speak the same language, and it's for that reason that the desert allows the crossing. It's going to test the caravan's every step to see if it's in time, and, if it is, we will make it to the oasis."

"If either of us had joined this caravan based only on personal courage, but without understanding that language, this journey would have been much more difficult."

They stood there looking at the moon.

"That's the magic of omens," said the boy. "I've seen how the guides read the signs of the desert, and how the soul of the caravan speaks to the soul of the desert."

The Englishman said, "I'd better pay more attention to the caravan."

"And I'd better read your books," said the boy.

* * *

They were strange books. They spoke about mercury, salt, dragons, and kings, and he didn't understand any of it. But there was one idea that seemed to repeat itself throughout all the books: all things are the manifestation of one thing only.

In one of the books he learned that the most important text in the literature of alchemy contained only a few lines, and had been inscribed on the surface of an emerald.

"It's the Emerald Tablet," said the Englishman, proud that he might teach something to the boy.

"Well, then, why do we need all these books?" the boy asked.

"So that we can understand those few lines," the Englishman answered, without appearing really to believe what he had said.

The book that most interested the boy told the stories of the famous alchemists. They were men who had dedicated their entire lives to the purification of metals in their laboratories; they believed that, if a metal were heated for many years, it would free itself of all its individual properties, and what was left would be the Soul of the World. This Soul of the World allowed them to understand anything on the face of the earth, because it was the language with which all things communicated. They called that discovery the Master Work—it was part liquid and part solid.

"Can't you just observe men and omens in order to understand the language?" the boy asked.

"You have a mania for simplifying everything," answered the Englishman, irritated. "Alchemy is a serious discipline. Every step has to be followed exactly as it was followed by the masters."

The boy learned that the liquid part of the Master Work was called the Elixir of Life, and that it cured all illnesses; it also kept the alchemist from growing old. And the solid part was called the Philosopher's Stone.

"It's not easy to find the Philosopher's Stone," said the Englishman. "The alchemists spent years in their laboratories, observing the fire that purified the metals. They spent so much time close to the fire that gradually they gave up the vanities of the world. They discovered that the purification of the metals had led to a purification of themselves."

The boy thought about the crystal merchant. He had said that it was a good thing for the boy to clean the crystal pieces, so that he could free himself from negative thoughts. The boy was becoming more and more convinced that alchemy could be learned in one's daily life.

"Also," said the Englishman, "the Philosopher's Stone has a fascinating property. A small sliver of the stone can transform large quantities of metal into gold."

Having heard that, the boy became even more interested in alchemy. He thought that, with some patience, he'd be able to transform everything into gold. He read the lives of the various people who had succeeded in doing so: Helvétius, Elias, Fulcanelli, and Geber. They were fascinating stories: each of them lived out his destiny to the end. They traveled, spoke with wise men, performed miracles for the incredulous, and owned the Philosopher's Stone and the Elixir of Life.

But when the boy wanted to learn how to achieve the Master Work, he became completely lost. There were just drawings, coded instructions, and obscure texts.

* * *

"Why do they make things so complicated?" he asked the Englishman one night. The boy had noticed that the Englishman was irritable, and missed his books.

"So that those who have the responsibility for understanding can understand," he said. "Imagine if everyone went around transforming lead into gold. Gold would lose its value.

"It's only those who are persistent, and willing to study things deeply, who achieve the Master Work. That's why I'm here in the middle of the desert. I'm seeking a true alchemist who will help me to decipher the codes."

"When were these books written?" the boy asked.

"Many centuries ago."

"They didn't have the printing press in those days," the boy argued. "There was no way for everybody to know about alchemy. Why did they use such strange language, with so many drawings?"

The Englishman didn't answer him directly. He said that for the past few days he had been paying attention to how the caravan operated, but that he hadn't learned anything new. The only thing he had noticed was that talk of war was becoming more and more frequent.

* * *

Then one day the boy returned the books to the Englishman. "Did you learn anything?" the Englishman asked, eager to hear what it might be. He needed someone to talk to so as to avoid thinking about the possibility of war.

"I learned that the world has a soul, and that whoever understands that soul can also understand the language of things. I learned that many alchemists realized their destinies, and wound up discovering the Soul of the World, the Philosopher's Stone, and the Elixir of Life.

"But, above all, I learned that these things are all so simple that they could be written on the surface of an emerald."

The Englishman was disappointed. The years of research, the magic symbols, the strange words and the laboratory equipment … none of this had made an impression on the boy. His soul must be too primitive to understand those things, he thought.

He took back his books and packed them away again in their bags.

"Go back to watching the caravan," he said. "That didn't teach me anything, either."

The boy went back to contemplating the silence of the desert, and the sand raised by the animals. "Everyone has his or her own way of learning things," he said to himself. "His way isn't the same as mine, nor mine as his. But we're both in search of our destinies, and I respect him for that."

* * *

The caravan began to travel day and night. The hooded Bedouins reappeared more and more frequently, and the camel driver — who had become a good friend of the boy's — explained that the war between the tribes had already begun. The caravan would be very lucky to reach the oasis.

The animals were exhausted, and the men talked among themselves less and less. The silence was the worst aspect of the night, when the mere groan of a camel — which before had been nothing but the groan of a camel — now frightened everyone, because it might signal a raid.

The camel driver, though, seemed not to be very concerned with the threat of war.

"I'm alive," he said to the boy, as they ate a bunch of dates one night, with no fires and no moon. "When I'm eating, that's all I think about. If I'm on the march, I just concentrate on marching. If I have to fight, it will be just as good a day to die as any other.

"Because I don't live in either my past or my future. I'm interested only in the present. If you can concentrate always on the present, you'll be a happy man. You'll see that there is life in the desert, that there are stars in the heavens, and that tribesmen fight because they are part of the human race. Life will be a party for you, a grand festival, because life is the moment we're living right now."

Two nights later, as he was getting ready to bed down, the boy looked for the star they followed every night. He thought that the horizon was a bit lower than it had been, because he seemed to see stars on the desert itself.

"It's the oasis," said the camel driver.

"Well, why don't we go there right now?" the boy asked.

"Because we have to sleep."

* * *

The boy awoke as the sun rose. There, in front of him, where the small stars had been the night before, was an endless row of date palms, stretching across the entire desert.

"We've done it!" said the Englishman, who had also awakened early.

But the boy was quiet. He was at home with the silence of the desert, and he was content just to look at the trees. He still had a long way to go to reach the pyramids, and someday this morning would just be a memory. But this was the present moment—the party the camel driver had mentioned—and he wanted to live it as he did the lessons of his past and his dreams of the future. Although the vision of the date palms would someday be just a memory, right now it signified shade, water, and a refuge from the war. Yesterday, the camel's groan signaled danger, and now a row of date palms could herald a miracle.

The world speaks many languages, the boy thought.

* * *

The times rush past, and so do the caravans, thought the alchemist, as he watched the hundreds of people and animals arriving at the oasis. People were shouting at the new arrivals, dust obscured the desert sun, and the children of the oasis were bursting with excitement at the arrival of the strangers. The alchemist saw the tribal chiefs greet the leader of the caravan, and converse with him at length.

But none of that mattered to the alchemist. He had already seen many people come and go, and the desert remained as it was. He had seen kings and beggars walking the desert sands. The dunes were changed constantly by the wind, yet these were the same sands he had known since he was a child. He always enjoyed seeing the happiness that the travelers experienced when, after weeks of yellow sand and blue sky, they first saw the green of the date palms. Maybe God created the desert so that man could appreciate the date trees, he thought.

He decided to concentrate on more practical matters. He knew that in the caravan there was a man to whom he was to teach some of his secrets. The omens had told him so. He didn't know the man yet, but his practiced eye would recognize him when he appeared. He hoped that it would be someone as capable as his previous apprentice.

I don't know why these things have to be transmitted by word of mouth, he thought. It wasn't exactly that they were secrets; God revealed his secrets easily to all his creatures.

He had only one explanation for this fact: things have to be transmitted this way because they were made up from the pure life, and this kind of life cannot be captured in pictures or words.

Because people become fascinated with pictures and words, and wind up forgetting the Language of the World.

* * *

The boy couldn't believe what he was seeing: the oasis, rather than being just a well surrounded by a few palm trees — as he had seen once in a geography book — was much larger than many towns back in Spain. There were three hundred wells, fifty thousand date trees, and innumerable colored tents spread among them.

"It looks like *The Thousand and One Nights*," said the Englishman, impatient to meet with the alchemist.

They were surrounded by children, curious to look at the animals and people that were arriving. The men of the oasis wanted to know if they had seen any fighting, and the women competed with one another for access to the cloth and precious stones brought by the merchants. The silence of the desert was a distant dream; the travelers in the caravan were talking incessantly, laughing and shouting, as if they had emerged from the spiritual world and found themselves once again in the world of people. They were relieved and happy.

They had been taking careful precautions in the desert, but the camel driver explained to the boy that oases were always considered to be neutral territories, because the majority of the inhabitants were women and children. There were oases throughout the desert, but the tribesmen fought in the desert, leaving the oases as places of refuge.

With some difficulty, the leader of the caravan brought all his people together and gave them his instructions. The group was to remain there at the oasis until the conflict between the tribes was over. Since they were visitors, they would have to share living space with those who lived there, and would be given the best accommodations. That was the law of hospitality. Then he asked that everyone, including his own sentinels, hand over their arms to the men appointed by the tribal chieftains.

"Those are the rules of war," the leader explained. "The oases may not shelter armies or troops."

To the boy's surprise, the Englishman took a chrome-plated revolver out of his bag and gave it to the men who were collecting the arms.

"Why a revolver?" he asked.

"It helped me to trust in people," the Englishman answered.

Meanwhile, the boy thought about his treasure. The closer he got to the realization of his dream, the more difficult things became. It seemed as if what the old king had called "beginner's luck" were no longer functioning. In his pursuit of the dream, he was being constantly subjected to tests of his persistence and courage. So he could not be hasty, nor impatient. If he pushed forward impulsively, he would fail to see the signs and omens left by God along his path.

God placed them along my path. He had surprised himself with the thought. Until then, he had considered the omens to be things of this world. Like eating or sleeping, or like seeking love or finding a job. He had never thought of them in terms of a language used by God to indicate what he should do.

"Don't be impatient," he repeated to himself. "It's like the camel driver said: 'Eat when it's time to eat. And move along when it's time to move along.'"

That first day, everyone slept from exhaustion, including the Englishman. The boy was assigned a place far from his friend, in a tent with five other young men of about his age. They were people of the desert, and clamored to hear his stories about the great cities.

The boy told them about his life as a shepherd, and was about to tell them of his experiences at the crystal shop when the Englishman came into the tent.

"I've been looking for you all morning," he said, as he led the boy outside. "I need you to help me find out where the alchemist lives."

First, they tried to find him on their own. An alchemist would probably live in a manner that was different from that of the rest of the people at the oasis, and it was likely that in his tent an oven was continuously burning. They searched everywhere, and found that the oasis was much larger than they could have imagined; there were hundreds of tents.

"We've wasted almost the entire day," said the Englishman, sitting down with the boy near one of the wells.

"Maybe we'd better ask someone," the boy suggested.

The Englishman didn't want to tell others about his reasons for being at the oasis, and couldn't make up his mind. But, finally, he agreed that the boy, who spoke better Arabic than he, should do so. The boy approached a woman who had come to the well to fill a goatskin with water.

"Good afternoon, ma'am. I'm trying to find out where the alchemist lives here at the oasis."

The woman said she had never heard of such a person, and hurried away. But before she fled, she advised the boy that he had better not try to converse with women who were dressed in black, because they were married women. He should respect tradition.

The Englishman was disappointed. It seemed he had made the long journey for nothing. The boy was also saddened; his friend was in pursuit of his destiny. And, when someone was in such pursuit, the entire universe made an effort to help him succeed — that's what the old king had said. He couldn't have been wrong.

"I had never heard of alchemists before," the boy said. "Maybe no one here has, either."

The Englishman's eyes lit up. "That's it! Maybe no one here knows what an alchemist is! Find out who it is who cures the people's illnesses!"

Several women dressed in black came to the well for water, but the boy would speak to none of them, despite the Englishman's insistence. Then a man approached.

"Do you know someone here who cures people's illnesses?" the boy asked.

"Allah cures our illnesses," said the man, clearly frightened of the strangers. "You're looking for witch doctors." He spoke some verses from the Koran, and moved on.

Another man appeared. He was older, and was carrying a small bucket. The boy repeated his question.

"Why do you want to find that sort of person?" the Arab asked.

"Because my friend here has traveled for many months in order to meet with him," the boy said.

"If such a man is here at the oasis, he must be the very powerful one," said the old man after thinking for a few moments. "Not even the tribal chieftains are able to see him when they want to. Only when he consents.

"Wait for the end of the war. Then leave with the caravan. Don't try to enter into the life of the oasis," he said, and walked away.

But the Englishman was exultant. They were on the right track.

Finally, a young woman approached who was not dressed in black. She had a vessel on her shoulder, and her head was covered by a veil, but her face was uncovered. The boy approached her to ask about the alchemist.

At that moment, it seemed to him that time stood still, and the Soul of the World surged within him. When he looked into her dark eyes, and saw that her lips were poised between a laugh and silence, he learned the most important part of the language that all the world spoke — the language that everyone on earth was capable of understanding in their heart. It was love. Something older than humanity, more ancient than the desert. Something that exerted the same force whenever two pairs of eyes met, as had theirs here at the well. She smiled, and that was certainly an omen—the omen he had been awaiting, without even knowing he was, for all his life. The omen he had sought to find with his sheep and in his books, in the crystals and in the silence of the desert.

It was the pure Language of the World. It required no explanation, just as the universe needs none as it travels through endless time. What the boy felt at that moment was that he was in the presence of the only woman in his life, and that, with no need for words, she recognized the same thing. He was more certain of it than of anything in the world. He had been told by his parents and grandparents that he must fall in love and really know a person before becoming committed. But maybe people who felt that way had never learned the universal language. Because, when you know that language, it's easy to understand that someone in the world awaits you, whether it's in the middle of the desert or in some great city. And when two such people encounter each other, and their eyes meet, the past and the future become unimportant. There is only that moment, and the incredible certainty that everything under the sun has been written by one hand only. It is the hand that evokes love, and creates a twin soul for every person in the world. Without such love, one's dreams would have no meaning.

Maktub, thought the boy.

The Englishman shook the boy: "Come on, ask her!"

The boy stepped closer to the girl, and when she smiled, he did the same.

"What's your name?" he asked.

"Fatima," the girl said, averting her eyes.

"That's what some women in my country are called."

"It's the name of the Prophet's daughter," Fatima said. "The invaders carried the name everywhere." The beautiful girl spoke of the invaders with pride.

The Englishman prodded him, and the boy asked her about the man who cured people's illnesses.

"That's the man who knows all the secrets of the world," she said. "He communicates with the genies of the desert."

The genies were the spirits of good and evil. And the girl pointed to the south, indicating that it was there the strange man lived. Then she filled her vessel with water and left.

The Englishman vanished, too, gone to find the alchemist. And the boy sat there by the well for a long time, remembering that one day in Tarifa the levanter had brought to him the perfume of that woman, and realizing that he had loved her before he even knew she existed. He knew that his love for her would enable him to discover every treasure in the world.

The next day, the boy returned to the well, hoping to see the girl. To his surprise, the Englishman was there, looking out at the desert.

"I waited all afternoon and evening," he said. "He appeared with the first stars of evening. I told him what I was seeking, and he asked me if I had ever transformed lead into gold. I told him that was what I had come here to learn.

"He told me I should try to do so. That's all he said: 'Go and try.'"

The boy didn't say anything. The poor Englishman had traveled all this way, only to be told that he should repeat what he had already done so many times.

"So, then try," he said to the Englishman.

"That's what I'm going to do. I'm going to start now."

As the Englishman left, Fatima arrived and filled her vessel with water.

"I came to tell you just one thing," the boy said. "I want you to be my wife. I love you."

The girl dropped the container, and the water spilled.

"I'm going to wait here for you every day. I have crossed the desert in search of a treasure that is somewhere near the Pyramids, and for me, the war seemed a curse. But now it's a blessing, because it brought me to you."

"The war is going to end someday," the girl said.

The boy looked around him at the date palms. He reminded himself that he had been a shepherd, and that he could be a shepherd again. Fatima was more important than his treasure.

"The tribesmen are always in search of treasure," the girl said, as if she had guessed what he was thinking. "And the women of the desert are proud of their tribesmen."

She refilled her vessel and left.

The boy went to the well every day to meet with Fatima. He told her about his life as a shepherd, about the king, and about the crystal shop. They became friends, and except for the fifteen minutes he spent with her, each day seemed that it would never pass. When he had been at the oasis for almost a month, the leader of the caravan called a meeting of all of the people traveling with him.

"We don't know when the war will end, so we can't continue our journey," he said. "The battles may last for a long time, perhaps even years. There are powerful forces on both sides, and the war is important to both armies. It's not a battle of good against evil. It's a war between forces that are fighting for the balance of power, and, when that type of battle begins, it lasts longer than others — because Allah is on both sides."

The people went back to where they were living, and the boy went to meet with Fatima that afternoon. He told her about the morning's meeting. "The day after we met," Fatima said, "you told me that you loved me. Then, you taught me something of the universal language and the Soul of the World. Because of that, I have become a part of you."

The boy listened to the sound of her voice, and thought it to be more beautiful than the sound of the wind in the date palms.

"I have been waiting for you here at this oasis for a long time. I have forgotten about my past, about my traditions, and the way in which men of the desert expect women to behave. Ever since I was a child, I have dreamed that the desert would bring me a wonderful present. Now, my present has arrived, and it's you."

The boy wanted to take her hand. But Fatima's hands held to the handles of her jug.

"You have told me about your dreams, about the old king and your treasure. And you've told me about omens. So now, I fear nothing, because it was those omens that brought you to me. And I am a part of your dream, a part of your destiny, as you call it.

"That's why I want you to continue toward your goal. If you have to wait until the war is over, then wait. But if you have to go before then, go on in pursuit of your dream. The dunes are changed by the wind, but the desert never changes. That's the way it will be with our love for each other.

"*Maktub*," she said. "If I am really a part of your dream, you'll come back one day."

The boy was sad as he left her that day. He thought of all the married shepherds he had known. They had a difficult time convincing their wives that they had to go off into distant fields. Love required them to stay with the people they loved.

He told Fatima that, at their next meeting.

"The desert takes our men from us, and they don't always return," she said. "We know that, and we are used to it. Those who don't return become a part of the clouds, a part of the animals that hide in the ravines and of the water that comes from the earth. They become a part of everything … they become the Soul of the World.

"Some do come back. And then the other women are happy because they believe that their men may one day return, as well. I used to look at those women and envy them their happiness. Now, I too will be one of the women who wait.

"I'm a desert woman, and I'm proud of that. I want my husband to wander as free as the wind that shapes the dunes. And, if I have to, I will accept the fact that he has become a part of the clouds, and the animals and the water of the desert."

The boy went to look for the Englishman. He wanted to tell him about Fatima. He was surprised when he saw that the Englishman had built himself a furnace outside his tent. It was a strange furnace, fueled by firewood, with a transparent flask heating on top. As the Englishman stared out at the desert, his eyes seemed brighter than they had when he was reading his books.

"This is the first phase of the job," he said. "I have to separate out the sulfur. To do that successfully, I must have no fear of failure. It was my fear of failure that first kept me from attempting the Master Work. Now, I'm beginning what I could have started ten years ago. But I'm happy at least that I didn't wait twenty years."

He continued to feed the fire, and the boy stayed on until the desert turned pink in the setting sun. He felt the urge to go out into the desert, to see if its silence held the answers to his questions.

He wandered for a while, keeping the date palms of the oasis within sight. He listened to the wind, and felt the stones beneath his feet. Here and there, he found a shell, and realized that the desert, in remote times, had been a sea. He sat on a stone, and allowed himself to become hypnotized by the horizon. He tried to deal with the concept of love as distinct from possession, and couldn't separate them. But Fatima was a woman of the desert, and, if anything could help him to understand, it was the desert.

As he sat there thinking, he sensed movement above him. Looking up, he saw a pair of hawks flying high in the sky.

He watched the hawks as they drifted on the wind. Although their flight appeared to have no pattern, it made a certain kind of sense to the boy. It was just that he couldn't grasp what it meant. He followed the movement of the birds, trying to read something into it. Maybe these desert birds could explain to him the meaning of love without ownership.

He felt sleepy. In his heart, he wanted to remain awake, but he also wanted to sleep. "I am learning the Language of the World, and everything in the world is beginning to make sense to me ... even the flight of the hawks," he said to himself. And, in that mood, he was grateful to be in love. When you are in love, things make even more sense, he thought.

Suddenly, one of the hawks made a flashing dive through the sky, attacking the other. As it did so, a sudden, fleeting image came to the boy: an army, with its swords at the ready, riding into the oasis. The vision vanished immediately, but it had shaken him. He had heard people speak of mirages, and had already seen some himself: they were desires that, because of their intensity, materialized over the sands of the desert. But he certainly didn't desire that an army invade the oasis.

He wanted to forget about the vision, and return to his meditation. He tried again to concentrate on the pink shades of the desert, and its stones. But there was something there in his heart that wouldn't allow him to do so.

"Always heed the omens," the old king had said. The boy recalled what he had seen in the vision, and sensed that it was actually going to occur.

He rose, and made his way back toward the palm trees. Once again, he perceived the many languages in the things about him: this time, the desert was safe, and it was the oasis that had become dangerous.

The camel driver was seated at the base of a palm tree, observing the sunset. He saw the boy appear from the other side of the dunes.

"An army is coming," the boy said. "I had a vision."

"The desert fills men's hearts with visions," the camel driver answered.

But the boy told him about the hawks: that he had been watching their flight and had suddenly felt himself to have plunged to the Soul of the World.

The camel driver understood what the boy was saying. He knew that any given thing on the face of the earth could reveal the history of all things. One could open a book to any page, or look at a person's hand; one could turn a card, or watch the flight of the birds ... whatever the thing observed, one could find a connection with his experience of the moment.

Actually, it wasn't that those things, in themselves, revealed anything at all; it was just that people, looking at what was occurring around them, could find a means of penetration to the Soul of the World.

The desert was full of men who earned their living based on the ease with which they could penetrate to the Soul of the World. They were known as seers, and they were held in fear by women and the elderly. Tribesmen were also wary of consulting them, because it would be impossible to be effective in battle if one knew that he was fated to die.

The tribesmen preferred the taste of battle, and the thrill of not knowing what the outcome would be; the future was already written by Allah, and what he had written was always for the good of man. So the tribesmen lived only for the present, because the present was full of surprises, and they had to be aware of many things: Where was the enemy's sword? Where was his horse? What kind of blow should one deliver next in order to remain alive? The camel driver was not a fighter, and he had consulted with seers. Many of them had been right about what they said, while some had been wrong. Then, one day, the oldest seer he had ever sought out (and the one most to be feared) had asked why the camel driver was so interested in the future.

"Well ... so I can do things," he had responded. "And so I can change those things that I don't want to happen."

"But then they wouldn't be a part of your future," the seer had said.

"Well, maybe I just want to know the future so I can prepare myself for what's coming."

"If good things are coming, they will be a pleasant surprise," said the seer. "If bad things are, and you know in advance, you will suffer greatly before they even occur."

"I want to know about the future because I'm a man," the camel driver had said to the seer. "And men always live their lives based on the future."

The seer was a specialist in the casting of twigs; he threw them on the ground, and made interpretations based on how they fell. That day, he didn't make a cast. He wrapped the twigs in a piece of cloth and put them back in his bag.

"I make my living forecasting the future for people," he said. "I know the science of the twigs, and I know how to use them to penetrate to the place where all is written. There, I can read the past, discover what has already been forgotten, and understand the omens that are here in the present.

"When people consult me, it's not that I'm reading the future; I am guessing at the future. The future belongs to God, and it is only he who reveals it, under extraordinary circumstances. How do I guess at the future? Based on the omens of the present. The secret is here in the present. If you pay attention to the present, you can improve upon it. And, if you improve on the present, what comes later will also be better. Forget about the future, and live each day according to the teachings, confident that God loves his children.

Each day, in itself, brings with it an eternity."

The camel driver had asked what the circumstances were under which God would allow him to see the future.

"Only when he, himself, reveals it. And God only rarely reveals the future. When he does so, it is for only one reason: it's a future that was written so as to be altered."

God had shown the boy a part of the future, the camel driver thought. Why was it that he wanted the boy to serve as his instrument?

"Go and speak to the tribal chieftains," said the camel driver. "Tell them about the armies that are approaching."

"They'll laugh at me."

"They are men of the desert, and the men of the desert are used to dealing with omens."

"Well, then, they probably already know."

"They're not concerned with that right now. They believe that if they have to know about something Allah wants them to know, someone will tell them about it. It has happened many times before. But, this time, the person is you."

The boy thought of Fatima. And he decided he would go to see the chiefs of the tribes.

* * *

The boy approached the guard at the front of the huge white tent at the center of the oasis.

"I want to see the chieftains. I've brought omens from the desert."

Without responding, the guard entered the tent, where he remained for some time. When he emerged, it was with a young Arab, dressed in white and gold. The boy told the younger man what he had seen, and the man asked him to wait there. He disappeared into the tent.

Night fell, and an assortment of fighting men and merchants entered and exited the tent. One by one, the campfires were extinguished, and the oasis fell as quiet as the desert. Only the lights in the great tent remained. During all this time, the boy thought about Fatima, and he was still unable to understand his last conversation with her.

Finally, after hours of waiting, the guard bade the boy enter. The boy was astonished by what he saw inside. Never could he have imagined that, there in the middle of the desert, there existed a tent like this one. The ground was covered with the most beautiful carpets he had ever walked upon, and from the top of the structure hung lamps of hand-wrought gold, each with a lighted candle. The tribal chieftains were seated at the back of the tent in a semicircle, resting upon richly embroidered silk cushions. Servants came and went with silver trays laden with spices and tea. Other servants maintained the fires in the hookahs. The atmosphere was suffused with the sweet scent of smoke.

There were eight chieftains, but the boy could see

immediately which of them was the most important: an Arab dressed in white and gold, seated at the center of the semicircle. At his side was the young Arab the boy had spoken with earlier.

"Who is this stranger who speaks of omens?" asked one of the chieftains, eyeing the boy.

"It is I," the boy answered. And he told what he had seen.

"Why would the desert reveal such things to a stranger, when it knows that we have been here for generations?" said another of the chieftains.

"Because my eyes are not yet accustomed to the desert," the boy said. "I can see things that eyes habituated to the desert might not see."

And also because I know about the Soul of the World, he thought to himself.

"The oasis is neutral ground. No one attacks an oasis," said a third chieftain.

"I can only tell you what I saw. If you don't want to believe me, you don't have to do anything about it."

The men fell into an animated discussion. They spoke in an Arabic dialect that the boy didn't understand, but, when he made to leave, the guard told him to stay. The boy became fearful; the omens told him that something was wrong. He regretted having spoken to the camel driver about what he had seen in the desert.

Suddenly, the elder at the center smiled almost imperceptibly, and the boy felt better. The man hadn't participated in the discussion, and, in fact, hadn't said a word up to that point. But the boy was already used to the Language of the World, and he could feel the vibrations of peace throughout the tent. Now his intuition was that he had been right in coming.

The discussion ended. The chieftains were silent for a few moments as they listened to what the old man was saying. Then he turned to the boy: this time his expression was cold and distant.

"Two thousand years ago, in a distant land, a man who believed in dreams was thrown into a dungeon and then sold as a slave," the old man said, now in the dialect the boy understood. "Our merchants bought that man, and brought him to Egypt. All of us know that whoever believes in dreams also knows how to interpret them."

The elder continued, "When the pharaoh dreamed of cows that were thin and cows that were fat, this man I'm speaking of rescued Egypt from famine. His name was Joseph. He, too, was a stranger in a strange land, like you, and he was probably about your age."

He paused, and his eyes were still unfriendly.

"We always observe the Tradition. The Tradition saved Egypt from famine in those days, and made the Egyptians the wealthiest of peoples. The Tradition teaches men how to cross the desert, and how their children should marry. The Tradition says that an oasis is neutral territory, because both sides have oases, and so both are vulnerable."

No one said a word as the old man continued.

"But the Tradition also says that we should believe the messages of the desert. Everything we know was taught to us by the desert."

The old man gave a signal, and everyone stood. The meeting was over. The hookahs were extinguished, and the guards stood at attention. The boy made ready to leave, but the old man spoke again.

"Tomorrow, we are going to break the agreement that says that no one at the oasis may carry arms. Throughout the entire day we will be on the lookout for our enemies. When the sun sets, the men will once again surrender their arms to me. For every ten dead men among our enemies, you will receive a piece of gold.

"But arms cannot be drawn unless they also go into battle. Arms are as capricious as the desert, and, if they are not used, the next time they might not function. If at least one of them hasn't been used by the end of the day tomorrow, one will be used on you."

When the boy left the tent, the oasis was illuminated only by the light of the full moon. He was twenty minutes from his tent, and began to make his way there.

He was alarmed by what had happened. He had succeeded in reaching through to the Soul of the World, and now the price for having done so might be his life. It was a frightening bet. But he had been making risky bets ever since the day he had sold his sheep to pursue his destiny. And, as the camel driver had said, to die tomorrow was no worse than dying on any other day. Every day was there to be lived or to mark one's departure from this world. Everything depended on one word: "*Maktub*."

Walking along in the silence, he had no regrets. If he died tomorrow, it would be because God was not willing to change the future. He would at least have died after having crossed the strait, after having worked in a crystal shop, and after having known the silence of the desert and Fatima's eyes. He had lived every one of his days intensely since he had left home so long ago. If he died tomorrow, he would already have seen more than other shepherds, and he was proud of that.

Suddenly he heard a thundering sound, and he was thrown to the ground by a wind such as he had never known. The area was swirling in dust so intense that it hid the moon from view. Before him was an enormous white horse, rearing over him with a frightening scream.

When the blinding dust had settled a bit, the boy trembled at what he saw. Astride the animal was a horseman dressed completely in black, with a falcon perched on his left shoulder. He wore a turban and his entire face, except for his eyes, was covered with a black kerchief. He appeared to be a messenger from the desert, but his presence was much more powerful than that of a mere messenger.

The strange horseman drew an enormous, curved sword from a scabbard mounted on his saddle. The steel of its blade glittered in the light of the moon.

"Who dares to read the meaning of the flight of the hawks?" he demanded, so loudly that his words seemed to echo through the fifty thousand palm trees of Al-Fayoum.

"It is I who dared to do so," said the boy. He was reminded of the image of Santiago Matamoros, mounted on his white horse, with the infidels beneath his hooves. This man looked exactly the same, except that now the roles were reversed.

"It is I who dared to do so," he repeated, and he lowered his head to receive a blow from the sword. "Many lives will be saved, because I was able to see through to the Soul of the World."

The sword didn't fall. Instead, the stranger lowered it slowly, until the point touched the boy's forehead. It drew a droplet of blood.

The horseman was completely immobile, as was the boy. It didn't even occur to the boy to flee. In his heart, he felt a strange sense of joy: he was about to die in pursuit of his destiny. And for Fatima. The omens had been true, after all. Here he was, face-to-face with his enemy, but there was no need to be concerned about dying—the Soul of the World awaited him, and he would soon be a part of it. And, tomorrow, his enemy would also be a part of that Soul.

The stranger continued to hold the sword at the boy's forehead. "Why did you read the flight of the birds?"

"I read only what the birds wanted to tell me. They wanted to save the oasis. Tomorrow all of you will die, because there are more men at the oasis than you have."

The sword remained where it was. "Who are you to change what Allah has willed?"

"Allah created the armies, and he also created the hawks. Allah taught me the language of the birds. Everything has been written by the same hand," the boy said, remembering the camel driver's words.

The stranger withdrew the sword from the boy's forehead, and the boy felt immensely relieved. But he still couldn't flee.

"Be careful with your prognostications," said the stranger. "When something is written, there is no way to change it."

"All I saw was an army," said the boy. "I didn't see the outcome of the battle."

The stranger seemed satisfied with the answer. But he kept the sword in his hand. "What is a stranger doing in a strange land?"

"I am following my destiny. It's not something you would understand."

The stranger placed his sword in its scabbard, and the boy relaxed.

"I had to test your courage," the stranger said. "Courage is the quality most essential to understanding the Language of the World."

The boy was surprised. The stranger was speaking of things that very few people knew about.

"You must not let up, even after having come so far," he continued. "You must love the desert, but never trust it completely. Because the desert tests all men: it challenges every step, and kills those who become distracted."

What he said reminded the boy of the old king.

"If the warriors come here, and your head is still on your shoulders at sunset, come and find me," said the stranger.

The same hand that had brandished the sword now held a whip. The horse reared again, raising a cloud of dust.

"Where do you live?" shouted the boy, as the horseman rode away.

The hand with the whip pointed to the south.

The boy had met the alchemist.

* * *

Next morning, there were two thosand armed men scattered throughout the palm trees at Al-Fayoum. Before the sun had reached its high point, five hundred tribesmen appeared on the horizon. The mounted troops entered the oasis from the north; it appeared to be a peaceful expedition, but they all carried arms hidden in their robes. When they reached the white tent at the center of Al-Fayoum, they withdrew their scimitars and rifles. And they attacked an empty tent.

The men of the oasis surrounded the horsemen from the desert and within half an hour all but one of the intruders were dead. The children had been kept at the other side of a grove of palm trees, and saw nothing of what had happened. The women had remained in their tents, praying for the safekeeping of their husbands, and saw nothing of the battle, either.

Paulo Coelho

Were it not for the bodies there on the ground, it would have appeared to be a normal day at the oasis.

The only tribesman spared was the commander of the battalion. That afternoon, he was brought before the tribal chieftains, who asked him why he had violated the Tradition. The commander said that his men had been starving and thirsty, exhausted from many days of battle, and had decided to take the oasis so as to be able to return to the war.

The tribal chieftain said that he felt sorry for the tribesmen, but that the Tradition was sacred. He condemned the commander to death without honor. Rather than being killed by a blade or a bullet, he was hanged from a dead palm tree, where his body twisted in the desert wind.

The tribal chieftain called for the boy, and presented him with fifty pieces of gold. He repeated his story about Joseph of Egypt, and asked the boy to become the counselor of the oasis.

* * *

When the sun had set, and the first stars made their appearance, the boy started to walk to the south. He eventually sighted a single tent, and a group of Arabs passing by told the boy that it was a place inhabited by genies. But the boy sat down and waited.

Not until the moon was high did the alchemist ride into view. He carried two dead hawks over his shoulder.

"I am here," the boy said.

"You shouldn't be here," the alchemist answered. "Or is it your destiny that brings you here?"

"With the wars between the tribes, it's impossible to cross the desert. So I have come here."

The alchemist dismounted from his horse, and signaled that the boy should enter the tent with him. It was a tent like many at the oasis. The boy looked around for the ovens and other apparatus used in alchemy, but saw none. There were only some books in a pile, a small cooking stove, and the carpets, covered with mysterious designs.

"Sit down. We'll have something to drink and eat these hawks," said the alchemist.

The boy suspected that they were the same hawks he had seen on the day before, but he said nothing. The alchemist lighted the fire, and soon a delicious aroma filled the tent. It was better than the scent of the hookahs.

"Why did you want to see me?" the boy asked.

"Because of the omens," the alchemist answered. "The wind told me you would be coming, and that you would need help."

"It's not I the wind spoke about. It's the other foreigner, the Englishman. He's the one that's looking for you."

"He has other things to do first. But he's on the right track. He has begun to try to understand the desert."

"And what about me?"

"When a person really desires something, all the universe conspires to help that person to realize his dream," said the alchemist, echoing the words of the old king. The boy understood. Another person was there to help him toward his destiny.

"So you are going to instruct me?"

"No. You already know all you need to know. I am only going to point you in the direction of your treasure."

"But there's a tribal war," the boy reiterated.

"I know what's happening in the desert."

"I have already found my treasure. I have a camel, I have my money from the crystal shop, and I have fifty gold pieces. In my own country, I would be a rich man."

"But none of that is from the Pyramids," said the alchemist.

"I also have Fatima. She is a treasure greater than anything else I have won."

"She wasn't found at the Pyramids, either."

They ate in silence. The alchemist opened a bottle and poured a red liquid into the boy's cup. It was the most delicious wine he had ever tasted.

"Isn't wine prohibited here?" the boy asked.

"It's not what enters men's mouths that's evil," said the alchemist. "It's what comes out of their mouths that is."

The alchemist was a bit daunting, but, as the boy drank the wine, he relaxed. After they finished eating they sat outside the tent, under a moon so brilliant that it made the stars pale.

"Drink and enjoy yourself," said the alchemist,

noticing that the boy was feeling happier. "Rest well tonight, as if you were a warrior preparing for combat. Remember that wherever your heart is, there you will find your treasure. You've got to find the treasure, so that everything you have learned along the way can make sense.

"Tomorrow, sell your camel and buy a horse. Camels are traitorous: they walk thousands of paces and never seem to tire. Then suddenly, they kneel and die. But horses tire bit by bit. You always know how much you can ask of them, and when it is that they are about to die."

*   *   *

The following night, the boy appeared at the alchemist's tent with a horse. The alchemist was ready, and he mounted his own steed and placed the falcon on his left shoulder. He said to the boy, "Show me where there is life out in the desert. Only those who can see such signs of life are able to find treasure."

They began to ride out over the sands, with the moon lighting their way. I don't know if I'll be able to find life in the desert, the boy thought. I don't know the desert that well yet.

He wanted to say so to the alchemist, but he was afraid of the man. They reached the rocky place where the boy had seen the hawks in the sky, but now there was only silence and the wind.

"I don't know how to find life in the desert," the

boy said. "I know that there is life here, but I don't know where to look."

"Life attracts life," the alchemist answered.

And then the boy understood. He loosened the reins on his horse, who galloped forward over the rocks and sand. The alchemist followed as the boy's horse ran for almost half an hour. They could no longer see the palms of the oasis—only the gigantic moon above them, and its silver reflections from the stones of the desert. Suddenly, for no apparent reason, the boy's horse began to slow.

"There's life here," the boy said to the alchemist. "I don't know the language of the desert, but my horse knows the language of life."

They dismounted, and the alchemist said nothing. Advancing slowly, they searched among the stones. The alchemist stopped abruptly, and bent to the ground. There was a hole there among the stones. The alchemist put his hand into the hole, and then his entire arm, up to his shoulder. Something was moving there, and the alchemist's eyes—the boy could see only his eyes—squinted with his effort. His arm seemed to be battling with whatever was in the hole. Then, with a motion that startled the boy, he withdrew his arm and leaped to his feet. In his hand, he grasped a snake by the tail.

The boy leapt as well, but away from the alchemist. The snake fought frantically, making hissing sounds that shattered the silence of the desert. It was a cobra, whose venom could kill a person in minutes.

"Watch out for his venom," the boy said. But even though the alchemist had put his hand in the hole, and had surely already been bitten, his expression was calm. "The alchemist is two hundred years old," the Englishman had told him. He must know how to deal with the snakes of the desert.

The boy watched as his companion went to his horse and withdrew a scimitar. With its blade, he drew a circle in the sand, and then he placed the snake within it. The serpent relaxed immediately.

"Not to worry," said the alchemist. "He won't leave the circle. You found life in the desert, the omen that I needed."

"Why was that so important?"

"Because the Pyramids are surrounded by the desert."

The boy didn't want to talk about the Pyramids. His heart was heavy, and he had been melancholy since the previous night. To continue his search for the treasure meant that he had to abandon Fatima.

"I'm going to guide you across the desert," the alchemist said.

"I want to stay at the oasis," the boy answered. "I've found Fatima, and, as far as I'm concerned, she's worth more than treasure."

"Fatima is a woman of the desert," said the alchemist. "She knows that men have to go away in order to return. And she already has her treasure: it's you. Now she expects that you will find what it is you're looking for."

"Well, what if I decide to stay?"

"Let me tell you what will happen. You'll be the counselor of the oasis. You have enough gold to buy many sheep and many camels. You'll marry Fatima, and you'll both be happy for a year. You'll learn to love the desert, and you'll get to know every one of the fifty thousand palms. You'll watch them as they grow, demonstrating how the world is always changing. And you'll get better and better at understanding omens, because the desert is the best teacher there is.

"Sometime during the second year, you'll remember about the treasure. The omens will begin insistently to speak of it, and you'll try to ignore them. You'll use your knowledge for the welfare of the oasis and its inhabitants. The tribal chieftains will appreciate what you do. And your camels will bring you wealth and power.

"During the third year, the omens will continue to speak of your treasure and your destiny. You'll walk around, night after night, at the oasis, and Fatima will be unhappy because she'll feel it was she who interrupted your quest. But you will love her, and she'll return your love. You'll remember that she never asked you to stay, because a woman of the desert knows that she must await her man. So you won't blame her. But many times you'll walk the sands of the desert, thinking that maybe you could have left ... that you could have trusted more in your love for Fatima. Because what kept you at the oasis was your own fear that you might never come back. At that point, the omens will tell you that your treasure is buried forever.

"Then, sometime during the fourth year, the omens will abandon you, because you've stopped listening to them. The tribal chieftains will see that, and you'll be dismissed from your position as counselor. But, by then, you'll be a rich merchant, with many camels and a great deal of merchandise. You'll spend the rest of your days knowing that you didn't pursue your destiny, and that now it's too late.

"You must understand that love never keeps a man from pursuing his destiny. If he abandons that pursuit, it's because it wasn't true love ... the love that speaks the Language of the World."

The alchemist erased the circle in the sand, and the snake slithered away among the rocks. The boy remembered the crystal merchant who had always wanted to go to Mecca, and the Englishman in search of the alchemist. He thought of the woman who had trusted in the desert. And he looked out over the desert that had brought him to the woman he loved.

They mounted their horses, and this time it was the boy who followed the alchemist back to the oasis. The wind brought the sounds of the oasis to them, and the boy tried to hear Fatima's voice.

But that night, as he had watched the cobra within the circle, the strange horseman with the falcon on his shoulder had spoken of love and treasure, of the women of the desert and of his destiny.

"I'm going with you," the boy said. And he immediately felt peace in his heart.

"We'll leave tomorrow before sunrise," was the
alchemist's only response.

* * *

The boy spent a sleepless night. Two hours before
dawn, he awoke one of the boys who slept in his tent,
and asked him to show him where Fatima lived. They
went to her tent, and the boy gave his friend enough
gold to buy a sheep.

Then he asked his friend to go into the tent where
Fatima was sleeping, and to awaken her and tell her
that he was waiting outside. The young Arab did as he
was asked, and was given enough gold to buy yet
another sheep.

"Now leave us alone," said the boy to the young
Arab. The Arab returned to his tent to sleep, proud to
have helped the counselor of the oasis, and happy at
having enough money to buy himself some sheep.

Fatima appeared at the entrance to the tent. The two
walked out among the palms. The boy knew that it
was a violation of the Tradition, but that didn't matter
to him now.

"I'm going away," he said. "And I want you to
know that I'm coming back. I love you because …"

"Don't say anything," Fatima interrupted. "One is
loved because one is loved. No reason is needed for
loving."

But the boy continued, "I had a dream, and I met with a king. I sold crystal and crossed the desert. And, because the tribes declared war, I went to the well, seeking the alchemist. So, I love you because the entire universe conspired to help me find you."

The two embraced. It was the first time either had touched the other.

"I'll be back," the boy said.

"Before this, I always looked to the desert with longing," said Fatima. "Now it will be with hope. My father went away one day, but he returned to my mother, and he has always come back since then."

They said nothing else. They walked a bit farther among the palms, and then the boy left her at the entrance to her tent.

"I'll return, just as your father came back to your mother," he said.

He saw that Fatima's eyes were filled with tears.

"You're crying?"

"I'm a woman of the desert," she said, averting her face. "But above all, I'm a woman."

Fatima went back to her tent, and, when daylight came, she went out to do the chores she had done for years. But everything had changed. The boy was no longer at the oasis, and the oasis would never again have the same meaning it had had only yesterday. It would no longer be a place with fifty thousand palm trees and three hundred wells, where the pilgrims arrived, relieved at the end of their long journeys. From that day on, the oasis would be an empty place for her.

From that day on, it was the desert that would be important. She would look to it every day, and would try to guess which star the boy was following in search of his treasure. She would have to send her kisses on the wind, hoping that the wind would touch the boy's face, and would tell him that she was alive. That she was waiting for him, a woman awaiting a courageous man in search of his treasure. From that day on, the desert would represent only one thing to her: the hope for his return.

* * *

"Don't think about what you've left behind," the alchemist said to the boy as they began to ride across the sands of the desert. "Everything is written in the Soul of the World, and there it will stay forever."

"Men dream more about coming home than about leaving," the boy said. He was already reaccustomed to desert's silence.

"If what one finds is made of pure matter, it will never spoil. And one can always come back. If what you had found was only a moment of light, like the explosion of a star, you would find nothing on your return."

The man was speaking the language of alchemy. But the boy knew that he was referring to Fatima.

It was difficult not to think about what he had left behind. The desert, with its endless monotony, put him to dreaming. The boy could still see the palm trees, the wells, and the face of the woman he loved. He could see the Englishman at his experiments, and the camel driver who was a teacher without realizing it. Maybe the alchemist has never been in love, the boy thought.

The alchemist rode in front, with the falcon on his shoulder. The bird knew the language of the desert well, and whenever they stopped, he flew off in search of game. On the first day he returned with a rabbit, and on the second with two birds.

At night, they spread their sleeping gear and kept their fires hidden. The desert nights were cold, and were becoming darker and darker as the phases of the moon passed. They went on for a week, speaking only of the precautions they needed to follow in order to avoid the battles between the tribes. The war continued, and at times the wind carried the sweet, sickly smell of blood. Battles had been fought nearby, and the wind reminded the boy that there was the language of omens, always ready to show him what his eyes had failed to observe.

On the seventh day, the alchemist decided to make camp earlier than usual. The falcon flew off to find game, and the alchemist offered his water container to the boy.

"You are almost at the end of your journey," said the alchemist. "I congratulate you for having pursued your destiny."

"And you've told me nothing along the way," said the boy. "I thought you were going to teach me some of the things you know. A while ago, I rode through the desert with a man who had books on alchemy. But I wasn't able to learn anything from them."

"There is only one way to learn," the alchemist answered. "It's through action. Everything you need to know you have learned through your journey. You need to learn only one thing more."

The boy wanted to know what that was, but the alchemist was searching the horizon, looking for the falcon.

"Why are you called the alchemist?"

"Because that's what I am."

"And what went wrong when other alchemists tried to make gold and were unable to do so?"

"They were looking only for gold," his companion answered. "They were seeking the treasure of their destiny, without wanting actually to live out the destiny."

"What is it that I still need to know?" the boy asked.

But the alchemist continued to look to the horizon. And finally the falcon returned with their meal. They dug a hole and lit their fire in it, so that the light of the flames would not be seen.

"I'm an alchemist simply because I'm an alchemist," he said, as he prepared the meal. "I learned the science from my grandfather, who learned from his father, and so on, back to the creation of the world. In those times, the Master Work could be written simply on an emerald. But men began to reject simple things, and to write tracts, interpretations, and philosophical studies. They also began to feel that they knew a better way than others had. Yet the Emerald Tablet is still alive today."

"What was written on the Emerald Tablet?" the boy wanted to know.

The alchemist began to draw in the sand, and completed his drawing in less than five minutes. As he drew, the boy thought of the old king, and the plaza where they had met that day; it seemed as if it had taken place years and years ago.

"This is what was written on the Emerald Tablet," said the alchemist, when he had finished.

The boy tried to read what was written in the sand.

"It's a code," said the boy, a bit disappointed. "It looks like what I saw in the Englishman's books."

"No," the alchemist answered. "It's like the flight of those two hawks; it can't be understood by reason alone. The Emerald Tablet is a direct passage to the Soul of the World.

"The wise men understood that this natural world is only an image and a copy of paradise. The existence of this world is simply a guarantee that there exists a world that is perfect. God created the world so that, through its visible objects, men could understand his spiritual teachings and the marvels of his wisdom. That's what I mean by action."

"Should I understand the Emerald Tablet?" the boy asked.

"Perhaps, if you were in a laboratory of alchemy, this would be the right time to study the best way to understand the Emerald Tablet. But you are in the desert. So immerse yourself in it. The desert will give you an understanding of the world; in fact, anything on the face of the earth will do that. You don't even have to understand the desert: all you have to do is contemplate a simple grain of sand, and you will see in it all the marvels of creation."

"How do I immerse myself in the desert?"

"Listen to your heart. It knows all things, because it came from the Soul of the World, and it will one day return there."

* * *

They crossed the desert for another two days in silence. The alchemist had become much more cautious, because they were approaching the area where the most violent battles were being waged. As they moved along, the boy tried to listen to his heart.

It was not easy to do; in earlier times, his heart had always been ready to tell its story, but lately that wasn't true. There had been times when his heart spent hours telling of its sadness, and at other times it became so emotional over the desert sunrise that the boy had to hide his tears. His heart beat fastest when it spoke to the boy of treasure, and more slowly when the boy stared entranced at the endless horizons of the desert. But his heart was never quiet, even when the boy and the alchemist had fallen into silence.

"Why do we have to listen to our hearts?" the boy asked, when they had made camp that day.

"Because, wherever your heart is, that is where you'll find your treasure."

"But my heart is agitated," the boy said. "It has its dreams, it gets emotional, and it's become passionate over a woman of the desert. It asks things of me, and it keeps me from sleeping many nights, when I'm thinking about her."

"Well, that's good. Your heart is alive. Keep listening to what it has to say."

During the next three days, the two travelers passed by a number of armed tribesmen, and saw others on the horizon. The boy's heart began to speak of fear. It told him stories it had heard from the Soul of the World, stories of men who sought to find their treasure and never succeeded. Sometimes it frightened the boy with the idea that he might not find his treasure, or that he might die there in the desert. At other times, it told the boy that it was satisfied: it had found love and riches.

"My heart is a traitor," the boy said to the alchemist, when they had paused to rest the horses. "It doesn't want me to go on."

"That makes sense," the alchemist answered. "Naturally it's afraid that, in pursuing your dream, you might lose everything you've won."

"Well, then, why should I listen to my heart?"

"Because you will never again be able to keep it quiet. Even if you pretend not to have heard what it tells you, it will always be there inside you, repeating to you what you're thinking about life and about the world."

"You mean I should listen, even if it's treasonous?"

"Treason is a blow that comes unexpectedly. If you know your heart well, it will never be able to do that to you. Because you'll know its dreams and wishes, and will know how to deal with them.

"You will never be able to escape from your heart. So it's better to listen to what it has to say. That way, you'll never have to fear an unanticipated blow."

The boy continued to listen to his heart as they crossed the desert. He came to understand its dodges and tricks, and to accept it as it was. He lost his fear, and forgot about his need to go back to the oasis, because, one afternoon, his heart told him that it was happy. "Even though I complain sometimes," it said, "it's because I'm the heart of a person, and people's hearts are that way. People are afraid to pursue their most important dreams, because they feel that they don't deserve them, or that they'll be unable to achieve them. We, their hearts, become fearful just thinking of loved ones who go away forever, or of moments that could have been good but weren't, or of treasures that might have been found but were forever hidden in the sands. Because, when these things happen, we suffer terribly."

"My heart is afraid that it will have to suffer," the boy told the alchemist one night as they looked up at the moonless sky.

"Tell your heart that the fear of suffering is worse than the suffering itself. And that no heart has ever suffered when it goes in search of its dreams, because every second of the search is a second's encounter with God and with eternity."

"Every second of the search is an encounter with God," the boy told his heart. "When I have been truly searching for my treasure, every day has been luminous, because I've known that every hour was a part of the dream that I would find it. When I have been truly searching for my treasure, I've discovered things along the way that I never would have seen had I not had the courage to try things that seemed impossible for a shepherd to achieve."

So his heart was quiet for an entire afternoon. That night, the boy slept deeply, and, when he awoke, his heart began to tell him things that came from the Soul of the World. It said that all people who are happy have God within them. And that happiness could be found in a grain of sand from the desert, as the alchemist had said. Because a grain of sand is a moment of creation, and the universe has taken millions of years to create it. "Everyone on earth has a treasure that awaits him," his heart said. "We, people's hearts, seldom say much about those treasures, because people no longer want to go in search of them. We speak of them only to children. Later, we simply let life proceed, in its own direction, toward its own fate. But, unfortunately, very few follow the path laid out for them—the path to their destinies, and to happiness. Most people see the world as a threatening place, and, because they do, the world turns out, indeed, to be a threatening place.

"So, we, their hearts, speak more and more softly. We never stop speaking out, but we begin to hope that our words won't be heard: we don't want people to suffer because they don't follow their hearts."

"Why don't people's hearts tell them to continue to follow their dreams?" the boy asked the alchemist.

"Because that's what makes a heart suffer most, and hearts don't like to suffer."

From then on, the boy understood his heart. He asked it, please, never to stop speaking to him. He asked that, when he wandered far from his dreams, his heart press him and sound the alarm. The boy swore that, every time he heard the alarm, he would heed its message.

That night, he told all of this to the alchemist. And the alchemist understood that the boy's heart had returned to the Soul of the World.

"So what should I do now?" the boy asked.

"Continue in the direction of the Pyramids," said the alchemist. "And continue to pay heed to the omens. Your heart is still capable of showing you where the treasure is."

"Is that the one thing I still needed to know?"

"No," the alchemist answered. "What you still need to know is this: before a dream is realized, the Soul of the World tests everything that was learned along the way. It does this not because it is evil, but so that we can, in addition to realizing our dreams, master the lessons we've learned as we've moved toward that dream. That's the point at which most people give up.

It's the point at which, as we say in the language of the desert, one 'dies of thirst just when the palm trees have appeared on the horizon.'

"Every search begins with beginner's luck. And every search ends with the victor's being severely tested."

The boy remembered an old proverb from his country. It said that the darkest hour of the night came just before the dawn.

* * *

On the following day, the first clear sign of danger appeared. Three armed tribesmen approached, and asked what the boy and the alchemist were doing there.

"I'm hunting with my falcon," the alchemist answered.

"We're going to have to search you to see whether you're armed," one of the tribesmen said.

The alchemist dismounted slowly, and the boy did the same.

"Why are you carrying money?" asked the tribesman, when he had searched the boy's bag.

"I need it to get to the Pyramids," he said.

The tribesman who was searching the alchemist's belongings found a small crystal flask filled with a liquid, and a yellow glass egg that was slightly larger than a chicken's egg.

"What are these things?" he asked.

"That's the Philosopher's Stone and the Elixir of Life. It's the Master Work of the alchemists. Whoever swallows that elixir will never be sick again, and a fragment from that stone turns any metal into gold."

The Arabs laughed at him, and the alchemist laughed along. They thought his answer was amusing, and they allowed the boy and the alchemist to proceed with all of their belongings.

"Are you crazy?" the boy asked the alchemist, when they had moved on. "What did you do that for?"

"To show you one of life's simple lessons," the alchemist answered. "When you possess great treasures within you, and try to tell others of them, seldom are you believed."

They continued across the desert. With every day that passed, the boy's heart became more and more silent. It no longer wanted to know about things of the past or future; it was content simply to contemplate the desert, and to drink with the boy from the Soul of the World. The boy and his heart had become friends, and neither was capable now of betraying the other.

When his heart spoke to him, it was to provide a stimulus to the boy, and to give him strength, because the days of silence there in the desert were wearisome. His heart told the boy what his strongest qualities were: his courage in having given up his sheep and in trying to live out his destiny, and his enthusiasm during the time he had worked at the crystal shop.

And his heart told him something else that the boy had never noticed: it told the boy of dangers that had threatened him, but that he had never perceived. His heart said that one time it had hidden the rifle the boy had taken from his father, because of the possibility that the boy might wound himself. And it reminded the boy of the day when he had been ill and vomiting out in the fields, after which he had fallen into a deep sleep. There had been two thieves farther ahead who were planning to steal the boy's sheep and murder him. But, since the boy hadn't passed by, they had decided to move on, thinking that he had changed his route.

"Does a man's heart always help him?" the boy asked the alchemist.

"Mostly just the hearts of those who are trying to realize their destinies. But they do help children, drunkards, and the elderly, too."

"Does that mean that I'll never run into danger?"

"It means only that the heart does what it can," the alchemist said.

One afternoon, they passed by the encampment of one of the tribes. At each corner of the camp were Arabs garbed in beautiful white robes, with arms at the ready. The men were smoking their hookahs and trading stories from the battlefield. No one paid any attention to the two travelers.

"There's no danger," the boy said, when they had moved on past the encampment.

The alchemist sounded angry: "Trust in your heart, but never forget that you're in the desert. When men are at war with one another, the Soul of the World can hear the screams of battle. No one fails to suffer the consequences of everything under the sun."

All things are one, the boy thought. And then, as if the desert wanted to demonstrate that the alchemist was right, two horsemen appeared from behind the travelers.

"You can't go any farther," one of them said. "You're in the area where the tribes are at war."

"I'm not going very far," the alchemist answered, looking straight into the eyes of the horsemen. They were silent for a moment, and then agreed that the boy and the alchemist could move along.

The boy watched the exchange with fascination. "You dominated those horsemen with the way you looked at them," he said.

"Your eyes show the strength of your soul," answered the alchemist.

That's true, the boy thought. He had noticed that, in the midst of the multitude of armed men back at the encampment, there had been one who stared fixedly at the two. He had been so far away that his face wasn't even visible. But the boy was certain that he had been looking at them.

Finally, when they had crossed the mountain range that extended along the entire horizon, the alchemist said that they were only two days from the Pyramids.

"If we're going to go our separate ways soon," the boy said, "then teach me about alchemy."

"You already know about alchemy. It is about penetrating to the Soul of the World, and discovering the treasure that has been reserved for you."

"No, that's not what I mean. I'm talking about transforming lead into gold."

The alchemist fell as silent as the desert, and answered the boy only after they had stopped to eat.

"Everything in the universe evolved," he said. "And, for wise men, gold is the metal that evolved the furthest. Don't ask me why; I don't know why. I just know that the Tradition is always right.

"Men have never understood the words of the wise. So gold, instead of being seen as a symbol of evolution, became the basis for conflict."

"There are many languages spoken by things," the boy said. "There was a time when, for me, a camel's whinnying was nothing more than whinnying. Then it became a signal of danger. And, finally, it became just a whinny again."

But then he stopped. The alchemist probably already knew all that.

"I have known true alchemists," the alchemist continued. "They locked themselves in their laboratories, and tried to evolve, as gold had. And they found the Philosopher's Stone, because they understood that when something evolves, everything around that thing evolves as well.

"Others stumbled upon the stone by accident. They already had the gift, and their souls were readier for such things than the souls of others. But they don't count. They're quite rare.

"And then there were the others, who were interested only in gold. They never found the secret. They

forgot that lead, copper, and iron have their own destinies to fulfill. And anyone who interferes with the
destiny of another thing never will discover his own."

The alchemist's words echoed out like a curse. He
reached over and picked up a shell from the ground.

"This desert was once a sea," he said.

"I noticed that," the boy answered.

The alchemist told the boy to place the shell over his
ear. He had done that many times when he was a
child, and had heard the sound of the sea.

"The sea has lived on in this shell, because that's its
destiny. And it will never cease doing so until the
desert is once again covered by water."

They mounted their horses, and rode out in the
direction of the Pyramids of Egypt.

* * *

The sun was setting when the boy's heart sounded
a danger signal. They were surrounded by gigantic
dunes, and the boy looked at the alchemist to see
whether he had sensed anything. But he appeared to
be unaware of any danger. Five minutes later, the boy
saw two horsemen waiting ahead of them. Before he
could say anything to the alchemist, the two horsemen
had become ten, and then a hundred. And then they
were everywhere in the dunes.

They were tribesmen dressed in blue, with black
rings surrounding their turbans. Their faces were hidden behind blue veils, with only their eyes showing.

Even from a distance, their eyes conveyed the strength of their souls. And their eyes spoke of death.

* * *

The two were taken to a nearby military camp. A soldier shoved the boy and the alchemist into a tent where the chief was holding a meeting with his staff.

"These are the spies," said one of the men.

"We're just travelers," the alchemist answered.

"You were seen at the enemy camp three days ago. And you were talking with one of the troops there."

"I'm just a man who wanders the desert and knows the stars," said the alchemist. "I have no information about troops or about the movement of the tribes. I was simply acting as a guide for my friend here."

"Who is your friend?" the chief asked. "An alchemist," said the alchemist. "He understands the forces of nature. And he wants to show you his extraordinary powers."

The boy listened quietly. And fearfully.

"What is a foreigner doing here?" asked another of the men.

"He has brought money to give to your tribe," said the alchemist, before the boy could say a word. And seizing the boy's bag, the alchemist gave the gold coins to the chief.

The Arab accepted them without a word. There was enough there to buy a lot of weapons.

"What is an alchemist?" he asked, finally.

"It's a man who understands nature and the world. If he wanted to, he could destroy this camp just with the force of the wind."

The men laughed. They were used to the ravages of war, and knew that the wind could not deliver them a fatal blow. Yet each felt his heart beat a bit faster. They were men of the desert, and they were fearful of sorcerers.

"I want to see him do it," said the chief.

"He needs three days," answered the alchemist. "He is going to transform himself into the wind, just to demonstrate his powers. If he can't do so, we humbly offer you our lives, for the honor of your tribe."

"You can't offer me something that is already mine," the chief said, arrogantly. But he granted the travelers three days.

The boy was shaking with fear, but the alchemist helped him out of the tent.

"Don't let them see that you're afraid," the alchemist said. "They are brave men, and they despise cowards."

But the boy couldn't even speak. He was able to do so only after they had walked through the center of the camp. There was no need to imprison them: the Arabs simply confiscated their horses. So, once again, the world had demonstrated its many languages: the desert only moments ago had been endless and free, and now it was an impenetrable wall.

"You gave them everything I had!" the boy said. "Everything I've saved in my entire life!"

"Well, what good would it be to you if you had to die?" the alchemist answered. "Your money saved us for three days. It's not often that money saves a person's life."

But the boy was too frightened to listen to words of wisdom. He had no idea how he was going to transform himself into the wind. He wasn't an alchemist!

The alchemist asked one of the soldiers for some tea, and poured some on the boy's wrists. A wave of relief washed over him, and the alchemist muttered some words that the boy didn't understand.

"Don't give in to your fears," said the alchemist, in a strangely gentle voice. "If you do, you won't be able to talk to your heart."

"But I have no idea how to turn myself into the wind."

"If a person is living out his destiny, he knows everything he needs to know. There is only one thing that makes a dream impossible to achieve: the fear of failure."

"I'm not afraid of failing. It's just that I don't know how to turn myself into the wind."

"Well, you'll have to learn; your life depends on it."

"But what if I can't?"

"Then you'll die in the midst of trying to realize your destiny. That's a lot better than dying like millions of other people, who never even knew what their destinies were.

"But don't worry," the alchemist continued. "Usually the threat of death makes people a lot more aware of their lives."

The first day passed. There was a major battle nearby, and a number of wounded were brought back to the camp. The dead soldiers were replaced by others, and life went on. Death doesn't change anything, the boy thought.

"You could have died later on," a soldier said to the body of one of his companions. "You could have died after peace had been declared. But, in any case, you were going to die."

At the end of the day, the boy went looking for the alchemist, who had taken his falcon out into the desert.

"I still have no idea how to turn myself into the wind," the boy repeated.

"Remember what I told you: the world is only the visible aspect of God. And that what alchemy does is to bring spiritual perfection into contact with the material plane."

"What are you doing?"

"Feeding my falcon."

"If I'm not able to turn myself into the wind, we're going to die," the boy said. "Why feed your falcon?"

"You're the one who may die," the alchemist said. "I already know how to turn myself into the wind."

* * *

On the second day, the boy climbed to the top of a cliff near the camp. The sentinels allowed him to go; they had already heard about the sorcerer who could turn himself into the wind, and they didn't want to go near him. In any case, the desert was impassable.

He spent the entire afternoon of the second day looking out over the desert, and listening to his heart. The boy knew the desert sensed his fear.

They both spoke the same language.

* * *

On the third day, the chief met with his officers. He called the alchemist to the meeting and said, "Let's go see the boy who turns himself into the wind."

"Let's," the alchemist answered.

The boy took them to the cliff where he had been on the previous day. He told them all to be seated.

"It's going to take a while," the boy said.

"We're in no hurry," the chief answered. "We are men of the desert."

The boy looked out at the horizon. There were mountains in the distance. And there were dunes, rocks, and plants that insisted on living where survival seemed impossible. There was the desert that he had wandered for so many months; despite all that time, he knew only a small part of it. Within that small part, he had found an Englishman, caravans, tribal wars, and an oasis with fifty thousand palm trees and three hundred wells.

"What do you want here today?" the desert asked him. "Didn't you spend enough time looking at me yesterday?"

"Somewhere you are holding the person I love," the boy said. "So, when I look out over your sands, I am also looking at her. I want to return to her, and I need your help so that I can turn myself into the wind."

"What is love?" the desert asked.

"Love is the falcon's flight over your sands. Because for him, you are a green field, from which he always returns with game. He knows your rocks, your dunes, and your mountains, and you are generous to him."

"The falcon's beak carries bits of me, myself," the desert said. "For years, I care for his game, feeding it with the little water that I have, and then I show him where the game is. And, one day, as I enjoy the fact that his game thrives on my surface, the falcon dives out of the sky, and takes away what I've created."

"But that's why you created the game in the first place," the boy answered. "To nourish the falcon. And the falcon then nourishes man. And, eventually, man will nourish your sands, where the game will once again flourish. That's how the world goes."

"So is that what love is?"

"Yes, that's what love is. It's what makes the game become the falcon, the falcon become man, and man, in his turn, the desert. It's what turns lead into gold, and makes the gold return to the earth."

"I don't understand what you're talking about," the desert said.

"But you can at least understand that somewhere in your sands there is a woman waiting for me. And that's why I have to turn myself into the wind."

The desert didn't answer him for a few moments. Then it told him, "I'll give you my sands to help the wind to blow, but, alone, I can't do anything. You have to ask for help from the wind."

A breeze began to blow. The tribesmen watched the boy from a distance, talking among themselves in a language that the boy couldn't understand.

The alchemist smiled.

The wind approached the boy and touched his face. It knew of the boy's talk with the desert, because the winds know everything. They blow across the world without a birthplace, and with no place to die.

"Help me," the boy said. "One day you carried the voice of my loved one to me."

"Who taught you to speak the language of the desert and the wind?"

"My heart," the boy answered.

The wind has many names. In that part of the world, it was called the sirocco, because it brought moisture from the oceans to the east. In the distant land the boy came from, they called it the levanter, because they believed that it brought with it the sands of the desert, and the screams of the Moorish wars. Perhaps, in the places beyond the pastures where his sheep lived, men thought that the wind came from Andalusia. But, actually, the wind came from no place at all, nor did it go to any place; that's why it was stronger than the desert. Someone might one day plant trees in the desert, and even raise sheep there, but never would they harness the wind.

"You can't be the wind," the wind said. "We're two very different things."

"That's not true," the boy said. "I learned the alchemist's secrets in my travels. I have inside me the winds, the deserts, the oceans, the stars, and everything created in the universe. We were all made by the same hand, and we have the same soul. I want to be like you, able to reach every corner of the world, cross the seas, blow away the sands that cover my treasure, and carry the voice of the woman I love."

"I heard what you were talking about the other day with the alchemist," the wind said. "He said that everything has its own destiny. But people can't turn themselves into the wind."

"Just teach me to be the wind for a few moments," the boy said. "So you and I can talk about the limitless possibilities of people and the winds."

The wind's curiosity was aroused, something that had never happened before. It wanted to talk about those things, but it didn't know how to turn a man into the wind. And look how many things the wind already knew how to do! It created deserts, sank ships, felled entire forests, and blew through cities filled with music and strange noises. It felt that it had no limits, yet here was a boy saying that there were other things the wind should be able to do.

"This is what we call love," the boy said, seeing that the wind was close to granting what he requested. "When you are loved, you can do anything in creation. When you are loved, there's no need at all to understand what's happening, because everything happens within you, and even men can turn themselves into the wind. As long as the wind helps, of course."

The wind was a proud being, and it was becoming irritated with what the boy was saying. It commenced to blow harder, raising the desert sands. But finally it had to recognize that, even making its way around the world, it didn't know how to turn a man into the wind. And it knew nothing about love.

"In my travels around the world, I've often seen people speaking of love and looking toward the heavens," the wind said, furious at having to acknowledge its own limitations. "Maybe it's better to ask heaven."

"Well then, help me do that," the boy said. "Fill this place with a sandstorm so strong that it blots out the sun. Then I can look to heaven without blinding myself."

So the wind blew with all its strength, and the sky was filled with sand. The sun was turned into a golden disk.

At the camp, it was difficult to see anything. The men of the desert were already familiar with that wind. They called it the *simum*, and it was worse than a storm at sea. Their horses cried out, and all their weapons were filled with sand.

On the heights, one of the commanders turned to the chief and said, "Maybe we had better end this!"

They could barely see the boy. Their faces were covered with the blue cloths, and their eyes showed fear.

"Let's stop this," another commander said.

"I want to see the greatness of Allah," the chief said, with respect. "I want to see how a man turns himself into the wind."

But he made a mental note of the names of the two men who had expressed their fear. As soon as the wind stopped, he was going to remove them from their commands, because true men of the desert are not afraid.

"The wind told me that you know about love," the boy said to the sun. "If you know about love, you must also know about the Soul of the World, because it's made of love."

"From where I am," the sun said, "I can see the Soul of the World. It communicates with my soul, and together we cause the plants to grow and the sheep to seek out shade. From where I am — and I'm a long way from the earth — I learned how to love. I know that if I came even a little bit closer to the earth, everything there would die, and the Soul of the World would no longer exist. So we contemplate each other, and we want each other, and I give it life and warmth, and it gives me my reason for living."

"So you know about love," the boy said.

"And I know the Soul of the World, because we have talked at great length to each other during this endless trip through the universe. It tells me that its greatest problem is that, up until now, only the minerals and vegetables understand that all things are one. That there's no need for iron to be the same as copper, or copper the same as gold. Each performs its own exact function as a unique being, and everything would be a symphony of peace if the hand that wrote all this had stopped on the fifth day of creation.

"But there was a sixth day," the sun went on.

"You are wise, because you observe everything from a distance," the boy said. "But you don't know about love. If there hadn't been a sixth day, man would not exist; copper would always be just copper, and lead just lead. It's true that everything has its destiny, but one day that destiny will be realized. So each thing has to transform itself into something better, and to acquire a new destiny, until, someday, the Soul of the World becomes one thing only."

The sun thought about that, and decided to shine more brightly. The wind, which was enjoying the conversation, started to blow with greater force, so that the sun would not blind the boy.

"This is why alchemy exists," the boy said. "So that everyone will search for his treasure, find it, and then want to be better than he was in his former life. Lead will play its role until the world has no further need for lead; and then lead will have to turn itself into gold.

"That's what alchemists do. They show that, when we strive to become better than we are, everything around us becomes better, too."

"Well, why did you say that I don't know about love?" the sun asked the boy.

"Because it's not love to be static like the desert, nor is it love to roam the world like the wind. And it's not love to see everything from a distance, like you do. Love is the force that transforms and improves the Soul of the World. When I first reached through to it, I thought the Soul of the World was perfect. But later, I could see that it was like other aspects of creation,

and had its own passions and wars. It is we who nourish the Soul of the World, and the world we live in will
be either better or worse, depending on whether we
become better or worse. And that's where the power of
love comes in. Because when we love, we always strive
to become better than we are."

"So what do you want of me?" the sun asked.

"I want you to help me turn myself into the wind,"
the boy answered.

"Nature knows me as the wisest being in creation,"
the sun said. "But I don't know how to turn you into
the wind."

"Then, whom should I ask?"

The sun thought for a minute. The wind was listening closely, and wanted to tell every corner of the
world that the sun's wisdom had its limitations. That
it was unable to deal with this boy who spoke the
Language of the World.

"Speak to the hand that wrote all," said the sun.

The wind screamed with delight, and blew harder
than ever. The tents were being blown from their ties
to the earth, and the animals were being freed from
their tethers. On the cliff, the men clutched at each other as they sought to keep from being blown away.

The boy turned to the hand that wrote all. As he did
so, he sensed that the universe had fallen silent, and he
decided not to speak.

A current of love rushed from his heart, and the
boy began to pray. It was a prayer that he had never
said before, because it was a prayer without words or

pleas. His prayer didn't give thanks for his sheep having found new pastures; it didn't ask that the boy be able to sell more crystal; and it didn't beseech that the woman he had met continue to await his return. In the silence, the boy understood that the desert, the wind, and the sun were also trying to understand the signs written by the hand, and were seeking to follow their paths, and to understand what had been written on a single emerald. He saw that omens were scattered throughout the earth and in space, and that there was no reason or significance attached to their appearance; he could see that not the deserts, nor the winds, nor the sun, nor people knew why they had been created. But that the hand had a reason for all of this, and that only the hand could perform miracles, or transform the sea into a desert ... or a man into the wind. Because only the hand understood that it was a larger design that had moved the universe to the point at which six days of creation had evolved into a Master Work.

The boy reached through to the Soul of the World, and saw that it was a part of the Soul of God. And he saw that the Soul of God was his own soul. And that he, a boy, could perform miracles.

* * *

The *simum* blew that day as it had never blown before. For generations thereafter, the Arabs recounted the legend of a boy who had turned himself into the wind, almost destroying a military camp, in defiance of the most powerful chief in the desert.

When the *simum* ceased to blow, everyone looked to the place where the boy had been. But he was no longer there; he was standing next to a sand-covered sentinel, on the far side of the camp.

The men were terrified at his sorcery. But there were two people who were smiling: the alchemist, because he had found his perfect disciple, and the chief, because that disciple had understood the glory of God.

The following day, the general bade the boy and the alchemist farewell, and provided them with an escort party to accompany them as far as they chose.

* * *

They rode for the entire day. Toward the end of the afternoon, they came upon a Coptic monastery. The alchemist dismounted, and told the escorts they could return to the camp.

"From here on, you will be alone," the alchemist said. "You are only three hours from the Pyramids."

"Thank you," said the boy. "You taught me the Language of the World."

"I only invoked what you already knew."

The alchemist knocked on the gate of the monastery. A monk dressed in black came to the gates. They spoke for a few minutes in the Coptic tongue, and the alchemist bade the boy enter.

"I asked him to let me use the kitchen for a while," the alchemist smiled.

They went to the kitchen at the back of the monastery. The alchemist lighted the fire, and the monk brought him some lead, which the alchemist placed in an iron pan. When the lead had become liquid, the alchemist took from his pouch the strange yellow egg. He scraped from it a sliver as thin as a hair, wrapped it in wax, and added it to the pan in which the lead had melted.

The mixture took on a reddish color, almost the color of blood. The alchemist removed the pan from the fire, and set it aside to cool. As he did so, he talked with the monk about the tribal wars.

"I think they're going to last for a long time," he said to the monk.

The monk was irritated. The caravans had been stopped at Giza for some time, waiting for the wars to end. "But God's will be done," the monk said.

"Exactly," answered the alchemist.

When the pan had cooled, the monk and the boy looked at it, dazzled. The lead had dried into the shape of the pan, but it was no longer lead. It was gold.

"Will I learn to do that someday?" the boy asked.

"This was my destiny, not yours," the alchemist answered. "But I wanted to show you that it was possible."

They returned to the gates of the monastery. There, the alchemist separated the disk into four parts.

"This is for you," he said, holding one of the parts out to the monk. "It's for your generosity to the pilgrims."

"But this payment goes well beyond my generosity," the monk responded.

"Don't say that again. Life might be listening, and give you less the next time."

The alchemist turned to the boy. "This is for you. To make up for what you gave to the general."

The boy was about to say that it was much more than he had given the general. But he kept quiet, because he had heard what the alchemist said to the monk.

"And this is for me," said the alchemist, keeping one of the parts. "Because I have to return to the desert, where there are tribal wars."

He took the fourth part and handed it to the monk. "This is for the boy. If he ever needs it."

"But I'm going in search of my treasure," the boy said. "I'm very close to it now."

"And I'm certain you'll find it," the alchemist said.

"Then why this?"

"Because you have already lost your savings twice. Once to the thief, and once to the general. I'm an old, superstitious Arab, and I believe in our proverbs. There's one that says, 'Everything that happens once can never happen again. But everything that happens twice will surely happen a third time.'" They mounted their horses.

* * *

"I want to tell you a story about dreams," said the alchemist.

The boy brought his horse closer.

"In ancient Rome, at the time of Emperor Tiberius, there lived a good man who had two sons. One was in the military, and had been sent to the most distant regions of the empire. The other son was a poet, and delighted all of Rome with his beautiful verses.

"One night, the father had a dream. An angel appeared to him, and told him that the words of one of his sons would be learned and repeated throughout the world for all generations to come. The father woke from his dream grateful and crying, because life was generous, and had revealed to him something any father would be proud to know.

"Shortly thereafter, the father died as he tried to save a child who was about to be crushed by the wheels of a chariot. Since he had lived his entire life in a manner that was correct and fair, he went directly to heaven, where he met the angel that had appeared in his dream.

"'You were always a good man,' the angel said to him. 'You lived your life in a loving way, and died with dignity. I can now grant you any wish you desire.'

"'Life was good to me,' the man said. 'When you appeared in my dream, I felt that all my efforts had been rewarded, because my son's poems will be read by men for generations to come. I don't want anything for myself. But any father would be proud of the fame achieved by one whom he had cared for as a child, and educated as he grew up. Sometime in the distant future, I would like to see my son's words.'

"The angel touched the man's shoulder, and they

were both projected far into the future. They were in an immense setting, surrounded by thousands of people speaking a strange language.

"The man wept with happiness.

"'I knew that my son's poems were immortal,' he said to the angel through his tears. 'Can you please tell me which of my son's poems these people are repeating?'

"The angel came closer to the man, and, with tenderness, led him to a bench nearby, where they sat down.

"'The verses of your son who was the poet were very popular in Rome,' the angel said. 'Everyone loved them and enjoyed them. But when the reign of Tiberius ended, his poems were forgotten. The words you're hearing now are those of your son in the military.'

"The man looked at the angel in surprise.

"'Your son went to serve at a distant place, and became a centurion. He was just and good. One afternoon, one of his servants fell ill, and it appeared that he would die. Your son had heard of a rabbi who was able to cure illnesses, and he rode out for days and days in search of this man. Along the way, he learned that the man he was seeking was the Son of God. He met others who had been cured by him, and they instructed your son in the man's teachings. And so, despite the fact that he was a Roman centurion, he converted to their faith. Shortly thereafter, he reached the place where the man he was looking for was visiting.'

"'He told the man that one of his servants was

gravely ill, and the rabbi made ready to go to his house with him. But the centurion was a man of faith, and, looking into the eyes of the rabbi, he knew that he was surely in the presence of the Son of God.'

"'And this is what your son said,' the angel told the man. 'These are the words he said to the rabbi at that point, and they have never been forgotten: "My Lord, I am not worthy that you should come under my roof. But only speak a word and my servant will be healed."'"

The alchemist said, "No matter what he does, every person on earth plays a central role in the history of the world. And normally he doesn't know it."

The boy smiled. He had never imagined that questions about life would be of such importance to a shepherd.

"Good-bye," the alchemist said.

"Good-bye," said the boy.

* * *

The boy rode along through the desert for several hours, listening avidly to what his heart had to say. It was his heart that would tell him where his treasure was hidden.

"Where your treasure is, there also will be your heart," the alchemist had told him.

But his heart was speaking of other things. With pride, it told the story of a shepherd who had left his flock to follow a dream he had on two different occasions. It told of destiny, and of the many men who had wandered in search of distant lands or beautiful women, confronting the people of their times with their preconceived notions. It spoke of journeys, discoveries, books, and change.

As he was about to climb yet another dune, his heart whispered, "Be aware of the place where you are brought to tears. That's where I am, and that's where your treasure is."

The boy climbed the dune slowly. A full moon rose again in the starry sky: it had been a month since he had set forth from the oasis. The moonlight cast shadows through the dunes, creating the appearance of a rolling sea; it reminded the boy of the day when that horse had reared in the desert, and he had come to know the alchemist. And the moon fell on the desert's silence, and on a man's journey in search of treasure.

When he reached the top of the dune, his heart leapt. There, illuminated by the light of the moon and the brightness of the desert, stood the solemn and majestic Pyramids of Egypt.

The boy fell to his knees and wept. He thanked God for making him believe in his destiny, and for leading him to meet a king, a merchant, an Englishman, and an alchemist. And above all for his having met a woman of the desert who had told him that love would never keep a man from his destiny.

If he wanted to, he could now return to the oasis, go back to Fatima, and live his life as a simple shepherd. After all, the alchemist continued to live in the desert, even though he understood the Language of the World, and knew how to transform lead into gold. He didn't need to demonstrate his science and art to anyone. The boy told himself that, on the way toward realizing his own destiny, he had learned all he needed to know, and had experienced everything he might have dreamed of.

But here he was, at the point of finding his treasure, and he reminded himself that no project is completed until its objective has been achieved. The boy looked at the sands around him, and saw that, where his tears had fallen, a scarab beetle was scuttling through the sand. During his time in the desert, he had learned that, in Egypt, the scarab beetles are a symbol of God.

Another omen! The boy began to dig into the dune. As he did so, he thought of what the crystal merchant had once said: that anyone could build a pyramid in his backyard. The boy could see now that he couldn't do so if he placed stone upon stone for the rest of his life.

Throughout the night, the boy dug at the place he had chosen, but found nothing. He felt weighted down by the centuries of time since the Pyramids had been built. But he didn't stop. He struggled to continue digging as he fought the wind, which often blew the sand back into the excavation. His hands were abraded and exhausted, but he listened to his heart. It had told him to dig where his tears fell.

As he was attempting to pull out the rocks he encountered, he heard footsteps. Several figures approached him. Their backs were to the moonlight, and the boy could see neither their eyes nor their faces.

"What are you doing here?" one of the figures demanded.

Because he was terrified, the boy didn't answer. He had found where his treasure was, and was frightened at what might happen.

"We're refugees from the tribal wars, and we need money," the other figure said. "What are you hiding there?"

"I'm not hiding anything," the boy answered.

But one of them seized the boy and yanked him back out of the hole. Another, who was searching the boy's bags, found the piece of gold.

"There's gold here," he said.

The moon shone on the face of the Arab who had seized him, and in the man's eyes the boy saw death.

"He's probably got more gold hidden in the ground."

They made the boy continue digging, but he found nothing. As the sun rose, the men began to beat the boy. He was bruised and bleeding, his clothing was torn to shreds, and he felt that death was near.

"What good is money to you if you're going to die? It's not often that money can save someone's life," the alchemist had said. Finally, the boy screamed at the men, "I'm digging for treasure!" And, although his mouth was bleeding and swollen, he told his attackers that he had twice dreamed of a treasure hidden near the Pyramids of Egypt.

The man who appeared to be the leader of the group

spoke to one of the others: "Leave him. He doesn't have anything else. He must have stolen this gold."

The boy fell to the sand, nearly unconscious. The leader shook him and said, "We're leaving."

But before they left, he came back to the boy and said, "You're not going to die. You'll live, and you'll learn that a man shouldn't be so stupid. Two years ago, right here on this spot, I had a recurrent dream, too. I dreamed that I should travel to the fields of Spain and look for a ruined church where shepherds and their sheep slept. In my dream, there was a sycamore growing out of the ruins of the sacristy, and I was told that, if I dug at the roots of the sycamore, I would find a hidden treasure. But I'm not so stupid as to cross an entire desert just because of a recurrent dream."

And they disappeared.

The boy stood up shakily, and looked once more at the Pyramids. They seemed to laugh at him, and he laughed back, his heart bursting with joy.

Because now he knew where his treasure was.

Epilogue

The boy reached the small, abandoned church just as night was falling. The sycamore was still there in the sacristy, and the stars could still be seen through the half-destroyed roof. He remembered the time he had been there with his sheep; it had been a peaceful night ... except for the dream.

Now he was here not with his flock, but with a shovel.

He sat looking at the sky for a long time. Then he took from his knapsack a bottle of wine, and drank some. He remembered the night in the desert when he had sat with the alchemist, as they looked at the stars and drank wine together. He thought of the many roads he had traveled, and of the strange way God had chosen to show him his treasure. If he hadn't believed in the significance of recurrent dreams, he would not have met the Gypsy woman, the king, the thief, or ... "Well, it's a long list. But the path was written in the omens, and there was no way I could go wrong," he said to himself.

He fell asleep, and when he awoke the sun was already high. He began to dig at the base of the sycamore.

"You old sorcerer," the boy shouted up to the sky. "You knew the whole story. You even left a bit of gold at the monastery so I could get back to this church. The monk laughed when he saw me come back in tatters. Couldn't you have saved me from that?"

"No," he heard a voice on the wind say. "If I had told you, you wouldn't have seen the Pyramids. They're beautiful, aren't they?"

The boy smiled, and continued digging. Half an hour later, his shovel hit something solid. An hour later, he had before him a chest of Spanish gold coins. There were also precious stones, gold masks adorned with red and white feathers, and stone statues embedded with jewels. The spoils of a conquest that the country had long ago forgotten, and that some conquistador had failed to tell his children about.

The boy took out Urim and Thummim from his bag. He had used the two stones only once, one morning when he was at a marketplace. His life and his path had always provided him with enough omens.

He placed Urim and Thummim in the chest. They were also a part of his new treasure, because they were a reminder of the old king, whom he would never see again.

It's true; life really is generous to those who pursue their destiny, the boy thought. Then he remembered that he had to get to Tarifa so he could give one-tenth of his treasure to the Gypsy woman, as he had promised. "Those Gypsies are really smart," he thought. Maybe it was because they moved around so much.

The wind began to blow again. It was the levanter, the wind that came from Africa. It didn't bring with it the smell of the desert, nor the threat of Moorish invasion. Instead, it brought the scent of a perfume he knew well, and the touch of a kiss—a kiss that came from far away, slowly, slowly, until it rested on his lips.

The boy smiled. It was the first time she had done that.

"I'm coming, Fatima," he said.

More about Paulo Coelho
and The Alchemist

Tarifa
Tanger

An Interview with Paulo Coelho

by Laura Sheahen, for Beliefnet

With several bestselling novels translated into dozens of languages, Brazilian author Paulo Coelho is one of the world's most popular spiritual writers. His books—including *The Alchemist*, *Manual of the Warrior of Light* and *Veronika Decides to Die*—tackle everything from love to magic to suicide to the meaning of life. In a phone interview from France, Coelho spoke with Beliefnet recently about the spiritual search—his own and his readers'.

In *The Alchemist*, you refer to the Soul of the World. What exactly is this? How is it tied to religion or spirituality?
Well, let's distinguish religion from spirituality. I am Catholic, so religion for me is a way of having discipline and collective worship with persons who share the same mystery.

But in the end all religions tend to point to the same light. In between the light and us, sometimes there are too many rules. The light is here and there are no rules to follow this light.

The alchemist character says that "everything has a soul" — including inanimate objects like rocks and water. Do you believe that?
I do believe that everything we see, everything that is in front of us is just the visible part of reality. We have the invisible part of reality, like emotions for example, like feelings. This is our perception of the world, but God is as William Blake said — in a grain of sand and in a flower. This energy is everywhere.

Are all souls the same? Or are human souls in any way different?
I believe everything is one thing only. That said, there are some questions in my life that I don't know ... I've stopped asking. At the very beginning of my life, I wanted to have answers for everything. And now I respect the fact that I can't have answers for everything.

So for this question I go to the mystery of it and say I don't know. I only know that I am alive and there is something that manifests in my life, that it is God and one day I am going to understand my life, probably in the day that I die, or afterwards. But I try to find good questions and not good answers.

You say we might know more "afterwards". You're saying you think certain things might happen in the afterlife?

We cannot know anything for sure. But I don't believe in time either. You say "when we die", but time is another of these things that we need to help ourselves to go through life, but it does not exist. I am talking to you, but the moment that I am talking to you, the universe is being created and destroyed. I am living out my past and future lives. Whatever I do now, even in this conversation, can affect all my past and future lives.

I do believe in life after death, but I also don't think that it's that important. What is important is to understand that we are also living this life after death now.

So we have to get rid of the notion of time?

We have to try to get rid of the notion of time. And when you have an intense contact of love with nature or another human being, like a spark, then you understand that there is no time and that everything is eternal.

It sounds like this idea probably helped you overcome your fear of not existing, which you describe in the introduction to *The Alchemist*.

Yes, of course there was this fear of death. And one day when I made a pilgrimage to Santiago de Compostela, I had to go through an exercise and I had to face my death.

Since then, I realize that death is not the end of life, but it is also my best friend. She is always sitting by my side, even while I am talking to you, looking to the mountains here with snow.

Your death is always sitting by your side?
By my side, sitting in the chair right in front of me. I see death as a beautiful woman.

What is she saying?
She is saying, "I am going to kiss you," and I say to her, "Not now, please." But she says, "OK, not now — but pay attention and try to get the best of every moment because I am going to take you." And I say, "OK, thank you for giving me the most important advice in life — to live your moment fully."

You mentioned that you're Catholic, but you've said elsewhere that your Jesuit upbringing was painful in some ways. What do you see as the value of, and problems with, organized religion?
The value is that they give you discipline and they give you collective worship and they give you humbleness towards the mysteries. The dangers is that every religion, including the Catholic one, says, "I have the ultimate truth." Then you start to rely on the priest, the mullah, the rabbi, or whoever, to be responsible for your acts. In fact, you are the only one who is responsible.

In your book *Veronika Decides to Die*, Veronika is bored with the sameness of every day. How can people break out of the sameness?

Once someone asked me, "What do you want to be your epitaph?" So I said, "Paulo Coehlo died while he was alive." The person said, "Why this epitaph? Everybody dies when he or she is alive." I said, "No, this is not true." The same pattern repeating and over again, you are not alive any more.

To die alive is to take risks. To pay your price. To do something that sometimes scares you but you should do because you may like or you may not like.

You also say people should watch for omens. Can you describe what you mean by omens?

Omens are the individual language in which God talks to you. My omens are not your omens.

They are this strange, but very individual language that guides you towards your own destiny. They are not logical. They talk to your heart directly.

The only way that you can learn any language is by making mistakes. I made my mistakes, but then I started to connect with the signs that guide me. This silent voice of God that leads me to the places where I should be.

The Alchemist **talks about the principle of favorability, which is sort of like "beginner's luck". What would you say to people who feel they have never experienced beginner's luck? People who feel that every time they try to move toward a dream, they're blocked?**

Try again [laughs]. Because when you're really close to what God meant you to be here, you are going to experience beginner's luck.

In *Eleven Minutes*, you want to bring sexuality and spirituality to a healthier place. How can this happen?

Well, by accepting that sex is a physical manifestation of God, and that is not a sin — it is a blessing. And then by understanding that except for two things that I consider to be really sick — rape and pedophilia — you are free to be creative. It's up to you, how you do this.

Sex was always surrounded by taboos, and I don't see it necessarily as a manifestation of evil. I think that sexuality is first and foremost the way that God chooses for us to be here on earth, to enjoy this energy of love in the physical plane.

So with a healthy understanding of sexuality you're helping God manifest himself in the world?

Absolutely. Not only understanding, but practising.

Author Biography: Paulo Coelho

Paulo was born in Rio in August 1947, the son of Pedro Queima Coelho de Souza, an engineer, and his wife Lygia, a homemaker. Early on, Paulo dreamed of an artistic career, something frowned upon in his middle-class household. In the austere surroundings of a strict Jesuit school, Paulo discovered his true vocation: to be a writer. Paulo's parents, however, had different plans for him. When their attempts to suppress his devotion to literature failed, they took it as a sign of mental illness. When Paulo was seventeen, his father had him committed to a mental institution, twice, where he endured sessions of electroconvulsive "therapy". His parents brought him back there once more after he became involved with a theatre group and started to work as a journalist.

Paulo was always a nonconformist and a seeker of the new. When, in the excitement of 1968, the guerrilla and hippy movements took hold in a Brazil ruled by a repressive military regime, Paulo embraced progressive politics and joined the peace and love generation. He sought spiritual experience, traveling all over Latin America in the footsteps of Carlos Castaneda. He worked in the theatre and dabbled in journalism, launching an alternative magazine called *2001*. He began to collaborate with music producer Raul Seixas as a lyricist, transforming the Brazilian rock scene. In 1973, Paulo and Raul joined the Alternative Society, an organization that defended the individual's right to free expression, and began publishing a series of comic strips, calling for more freedom. Members of the organization were detained and imprisoned. Two days later, Paulo was kidnapped and tortured by a group of paramilitaries.

This experience affected him profoundly. At the age of 26, Paulo decided that he had had enough of living on the edge and wanted to be "normal". He worked as an executive in the music industry. He tried his hand at writing but didn't start seriously until after he had an encounter with a stranger. The man first came to him in a vision, and two months later Paulo met him at a café in Amsterdam. The stranger suggested that Paulo should return to Catholicism and study the benign side of magic. He also encouraged Paulo to walk the Road to Santiago, the medieval pilgrim's route.

In 1987, a year after completing that pilgrimage, Paulo wrote *The Pilgrimage*. The book describes his experiences and his discovery that the extraordinary occurs in the lives of ordinary people. A year later, Paulo wrote a very different book, *The Alchemist*. The first edition sold only 900 copies and the publishing house decided not to reprint.

Paulo would not surrender his dream. He found another publishing house, a bigger one. He wrote *Brida*, which received a lot of attention in the press, and both

The Alchemist and *The Pilgrimage* appeared on bestseller lists. *The Alchemist* went on to sell more copies than any other book in Brazilian literary history.

Paulo's story doesn't end there. He has gone on to write many other bestselling books that have touched the hearts of people everywhere: *The Valkyries, By the River Piedra I Sat Down and Wept, The Fifth Mountain, The Pilgrimage, Veronika Decides to Die, The Devil and Miss Prym, Manual of the Warrior of Light, Eleven Minutes, The Zahir, Like the Flowing River, The Witch of Portobello, Brida, The Winner Stands Alone, Aleph* and *Manuscript Found in Accra.*

On questions that
have no answers

On the mysterious path that connects a book to its reader, the presence of enthusiasts is fundamental, for they carry the writer's words onwards. So I want to thank all the enthusiasts of *The Alchemist* for making it possible for Santiago, the shepherd of the novel, to continue along the road through the beautiful landscapes of the world.

And I take this opportunity to tell a story: I often practise meditation using a bow and arrow (a Japanese technique called *kyudo*). Once, when I was in France, I climbed a path looking for a place where I could perform this type of active meditation and found myself in a small army camp. The soldiers there studied me, but I acted as if I didn't see them (we are all a little paranoid of being thought a spy), and continued on my way.

I found an ideal spot, and began my preparatory breathing exercises. It was then that I saw an armoured vehicle approaching.

I immediately went on the defensive, preparing my answers to whatever questions the soldiers might ask me: I have permission to use the bow ... It's a safe place ... Any objection to my being there should come from the forest rangers, not the army, etc. But a colonel stepped from the vehicle, and asked whether I was the author of *The Alchemist*.

When I answered that I was, he overcame his obvious timidity and told me a bit about himself.

He and his wife made donations in support of a child with leprosy. The child was originally from India, but had been brought to France. One day, curious to know more about the girl, they had gone to the convent where the nuns took responsibility for her care. The couple spent a beautiful afternoon there, and as they were preparing to leave, the Mother Superior asked that they help their adoptive daughter to understand more about life. The colonel replied that he had no experience other than his own. But that night, he prayed to God to help him.

In his dreams, an angel answered him: 'Rather than provide answers, try to learn what it is that children want to ask.'

When he awoke, the colonel resolved that he would visit some schools and have the students write down for him everything they would like to know about life. He asked that their questions be prepared in writing, wanting to avoid the possibility that the more timid children would be fearful of expressing themselves. The results showed that, no matter what our experience and background, we all have the same questions as those children.

For example:

Where do we go when we die?

Why are we frightened of strangers?

Why do accidents happen, even to those who believe in God?

Why are we born, when, in the end, we all die?

How many stars are there in the sky?

Does the Lord listen to those who do not believe in him?

Why does poverty and sickness exist?

Why did God create mosquitoes and flies?

Why does our guardian angel not come to us when we are sad?

Why do we love some people and hate others?

If God is in heaven, and my mother is also there because she died, how can He be alive?

Twenty-five years ago, when I wrote *The Alchemist*, I was trying to understand something of the reason for our existence. And, rather than prepare a philosophical treatise, I decided to talk to the child that existed in my soul.

To my surprise, that child is still alive in millions of people all over the world. The book has been translated into dozens of languages and published in more than 168 countries, helping me to share with other readers the questions that, precisely because they do not have answers, make life a wonderful adventure.

MANUSCRIPT
FOUND IN
ACCRA

The new international bestseller from
Paulo Coelho.

After lying undiscovered for over 700 years, a
manuscript holding the answers to a city's final
questions is unearthed. Centuries before, on the
eve of the invasion of Accra, the citizens had
gathered, and a man had stood before them and
invited the people to share their fears, that he
might offer hope and comfort. His extraordinary
insights on courage, solitude, loyalty and loss
were transcribed and passed on.

A timeless and powerful exploration of personal
growth, everyday wisdom and joy.

Read the excerpt now.

Preface and Greeting

In December 1945, two brothers looking for a place to rest found an urn full of papyruses in a cave in the region of Hamra Dom, in Upper Egypt. Instead of telling the local authorities – as the law demanded – they decided to sell them singly in the market for antiquities, thus avoiding attracting the government's attention. The boys' mother, fearing 'negative energies', burned several of the newly discovered papyruses.

The following year, for reasons history does not record, the brothers quarrelled. Attributing this quarrel to those supposed 'negative energies', the mother handed over the manuscripts to a priest, who sold them to the Coptic Museum in Cairo. There, the papyruses were given the name they still bear to this day: Manuscripts from Nag Hammadi (a reference to the town nearest to the caves where they were found). One of the museum's experts, the religious historian Jean Doresse, realised the importance of the discovery and mentioned it for the first time in a publication dated 1948.

Other papyruses began to appear on the black market. The Egyptian government tried to prevent the manuscripts from leaving the country. After the 1952 revolution, most of the material was handed over to the Coptic Museum in Cairo and declared part of the national heritage. Only one text eluded them, and this had turned up in an antiquarian shop in Belgium. After vain attempts to sell it in New York and Paris, it was finally acquired by the Carl Jung Institute in 1951. On the death of the famous psychoanalyst, the papyrus, now known as Jung Codex, returned to Cairo, where the almost one thousand pages and fragments of the Manuscripts from Nag Hammadi are now to be found.

* * *

The papyruses are Greek translations of texts written between the end of the first century BC and AD 180, and they constitute a body of work also known as the Apocryphal Gospels, because they are not included in the Bible as we know it today. Now why is that?

In AD 170, a group of bishops met to decide which texts would form part of the New Testament. The criterion was simple enough: anything that could be used to combat the heresies and doctrinal divisions of the age would be included. The four gospels we know today were chosen, as were the letters from the apostles and whatever else was judged to be, shall we say, 'coherent' with what the bishops believed to be the main tenets of Christianity. Reference to this meeting of the bishops and their list of authorised books can be found in the Muratorian Canon. The other books, like those found in Nag Hammadi, were omitted, either because they were written by women (for example, the Gospel according to Mary Magdalene) or because they depicted a Jesus who was aware of his divine mission and whose passage through death would, therefore, be less drawn out and painful.

* * *

In 1974, the English archaeologist Sir Walter Wilkinson discovered another manuscript, this time written in three languages: Arabic, Hebrew and Latin. Conscious of the laws protecting such finds in the region, he sent the text to the Department of Antiquities in the Museum of Cairo. Shortly afterwards, back came a response: there were at least 155 copies of the document circulating in the world (three of which belonged to the museum) and they were all practically identical. Carbon-14 tests (used to determine the age of organic matter) revealed that the document was relatively recent, possibly as late as 1307. It was easy enough to trace its origin to the city of Accra, outside Egyptian territory. There were, therefore, no restrictions on its removal from the country, and Sir Walter received written permission from the Egyptian government (Ref. 1901/317/IFP-75, dated 23 November 1974) to take it back to England with him.

* * *

I met Sir Walter's son in 1982, at Christmas, in Porthmadog in Wales. I remember him mentioning the manuscript discovered by his father, but neither of us gave much importance to the matter. We maintained a cordial relationship over the years and met on at least two other occasions when I visited Wales to promote my books.

On 30 November 2011, I received a copy of the text he had mentioned at that first meeting. I transcribe it here.

I would so like to begin by writing:

'Now that I am at the end of my life,
I leave for those who come after me
everything that I learned while I walked
the face of this Earth. May they make
good use of it.'

Alas, that is not true. I am only twenty-one, my parents gave me love and an education, and I married a woman I love and who loves me in return. However, tomorrow, life will undertake to separate us, and we must each set off in search of our own path, our own destiny or our own way of facing death.

As far as our family is concerned, today is the fourteenth of July 1099. For the family of Yakob, the childhood friend with whom I used to play in this city of Jerusalem, it is the year 4859 – he always takes great pride in telling me that Judaism is a far older religion than mine. For the worthy Ibn al-Athir, who spent his life trying to record a history that is now coming to a conclusion, the year 492 is about to end. We do not agree about dates or about the best way to worship God, but in every other respect we live together in peace.

A week ago, our commanders held a meeting. The French soldiers are infinitely superior and far better equipped than ours. We were given a choice: to abandon the city or fight to the death, because we will certainly be defeated. Most of us decided to stay.

The Muslims are, at this moment, gathered at the Al-Aqsa Mosque, while the Jews choose to assemble their soldiers in Mihrab Dawud – the Tower of David –

and the Christians, who live in various different quarters, have been charged with defending the southern part of the city.

Outside, we can already see the siege towers built from the enemy's dismantled ships. Judging from the enemy's movements, we assume that they will attack tomorrow morning, spilling our blood in the name of the Pope, the 'liberation' of the city and the 'divine will'.

This evening, in the same square where, a millennium ago, the Roman governor, Pontius Pilate, handed Jesus over to the mob to be crucified, a group of men and women of all ages went to see the Greek, whom we all know as the Copt.

The Copt is a strange man. As an adolescent, he decided to leave his native city of Athens to go in search of money and adventure. He ended up, close to starvation, knocking on the doors of our city, and, when he was well received, he gradually abandoned the idea of continuing his journey and resolved to stay.

He managed to find work in a shoemaker's shop and – just like Ibn al-Athir – he started recording everything he saw and heard for posterity. He did not seek to join any particular religion, and no one tried to persuade him otherwise. As far as he is concerned, we are not in the year 1099 or 4859, much less at the end of 492. The Copt believes only in the present moment and what he calls Moira – the unknown god, the Divine Energy, responsible for a single law, which, if ever broken, will bring about the end of the world.

Alongside the Copt were the patriarchs of the three religions that had settled in Jerusalem. No government official was present during this conversation; they were too preoccupied with making the final preparations for a resistance that we believe will prove utterly pointless.

'Many centuries ago, a man was judged and condemned in this square,' the Greek said. 'On the road to the right, while he was walking towards his death, he passed a group of women. When he saw them weeping, he said: "Weep not for me, weep for Jerusalem." He prophesied what is happening now. From tomorrow, harmony will become discord. Joy will be replaced by grief. Peace will give way to a war that will last into an unimaginably distant future.'

No one said anything, because none of us knew exactly why we were there. Would we have to listen to yet another sermon about these invaders who call themselves 'crusaders'? For a moment, the Copt appeared to savour the general confusion. And then, after a long silence, he explained:

'They can destroy the city, but they cannot destroy everything the city has taught us, which is why it is vital that this knowledge does not suffer the same fate as our walls, houses and streets. But what is knowledge?'

When no one replied, he went on:

'It isn't the absolute truth about life and death, but the thing that helps us to live and confront the challenges of day-to-day life. It isn't what we learn from books, which serves only to fuel futile arguments about what happened or will happen; it is the knowledge that lives in the hearts of men and women of good will.'

The Copt said:

'I am a learned man and yet, despite having spent all these years restoring antiquities, classifying objects, recording dates and discussing politics, I still don't know quite what to say to you. But I will ask the Divine Energy to purify my heart. You will ask me questions and I will answer them. That is what the teachers of

Ancient Greece did; their disciples would ask them questions about problems they had not yet considered, and the teachers would answer them.'

'And what shall we do with your answers?' someone asked.

'Some will write down what I say. Others will remember my words. The important thing is that tonight you will set off for the four corners of the world, telling others what you have heard. That way, the soul of Jerusalem will be preserved. And one day we will be able to rebuild Jerusalem, not just as a city, but as a centre of knowledge and a place where peace will once again reign.'

'We all know what awaits us tomorrow,' said another man. 'Wouldn't it be better to discuss how to negotiate for peace or prepare ourselves for battle?'

The Copt looked at the other religious men beside him and then immediately turned back to the crowd.

'None of us can know what tomorrow will hold, because each day has its good and its bad moments. So, when you ask your questions, forget about the troops outside and the fear inside. Our task is not to leave a record of what happened on this date for those who will inherit the Earth; history will take care of that. We will speak, therefore, about our daily lives, about the difficulties we have had to face. That is all the future will be interested in, because I do not believe very much will change in the next thousand years.'

Translated by Margaret Jull Costa

Life is a
journey

Make sure you don't miss a thing.
Live it with Paulo Coelho.

How can you find your heart's desire?

A world-wide phenomenon; an inspiration for anyone seeking their path in life.

The Alchemist

Do you believe in yourself?

A modern-day adventure in the searing heat of the Mojave desert and an exploration of fear and self-doubt.

The Valkyries

How do we see the amazing in every day?

When two young lovers are reunited, they discover anew the truth of what lies in their hearts.

By the River Piedra I Sat Down and Wept

What are you searching for?

A transforming journey on the pilgrims' road to Santiago – and the first of Paulo's extraordinary books.

The Pilgrimage

Can faith triumph over suffering?

Paulo Coelho's brilliant telling of the story of Elijah, who was forced to choose between love and duty.

The Fifth Mountain

Is life always worth living?

A fundamental moral question explored as only Paulo Coelho can.

Veronika Decides to Die

Could you be tempted into evil?

The inhabitants of a small town are challenged by a mysterious stranger to choose between good and evil.

The Devil and Miss Prym

Are you brave enough to live your dream?

Strategies and inspiration to help you follow your own path in a troubled world.

Manual of the Warrior of Light

Can sex be sacred?

An unflinching exploration of the lengths we go to in our search for love, sex and spirituality.

Eleven Minutes

How far would you go for your obsession?

A sweeping story of love, loss and longing that spans the world.

The Zahir

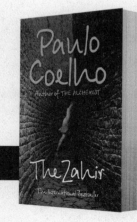

What does it mean to be truly alive?

Powerful tales of living and dying, destiny and choice and love lost and found.

Like the Flowing River

Can we dare to be true to ourselves?

A story that will transform the way we think about love, joy and sacrifice.

The Witch of Portobello

How will you know who your soulmate is?

A moving tale of passion, mystery and spirituality.

Brida

What happens when obsession turns to murder?

An enthralling story of jealousy, death and suspense.

The Winner Stands Alone

Are you where you want to be?

Read *Aleph*. And rewrite your life.

Aleph

Is there a weapon more powerful than words?

A timeless and powerful exploration of personal growth, everyday wisdom and joy.

Manuscript Found in Accra